destination
known

Drue Heinz Literature Prize 2001

destination known

BRETT ELLEN BLOCK

University of Pittsburgh Press

Published by the University of Pittsburgh Press, Pittsburgh, Pa. 15261

Manufactured in the United States of America

Printed on acid-free paper

10 9 8 7 6 5 4 3 2 1

Acknowledgments will be found at the end of the book.

ISBN 0-8229-4168-6

For my mother and father

Contents

destination known

Destination Known

IT WAS NOON and Margaret was sitting in her car in a parking lot watching a teenage boy dig through a dumpster. She had convinced herself that by the time he found whatever he was looking for she would be able to start the car and drive home. Ever since her apartment had been robbed, she'd begun having these moments where she would freeze up, like a window jammed in its frame, and today thirty minutes had already slipped by in that way. This time it started while she was in the hardware store. She had laid five different types of locks out on the counter and the clerk, who mistook her anxiety for indecision, had told her, "Just buy two. Hell, buy three. It'll make you feel better." Margaret bought all of them.

The July sun beat down on her car, and even with the windows open the heat was getting to her. Patches of tar on the parking lot were glistening in the sun. The teenage boy she was using as a sort of timer had fished a sandwich out of the dumpster and begun to eat it. He was wearing a black T-shirt and a dog collar around his neck. As he ate, he leaned over the rim of the dumpster casually, as if what he was doing were perfectly normal.

No matter how bad things got, Margaret thought she could never resort to something so depressing as searching a dumpster for a meal. But as she watched the boy eat, she considered that it was more a matter of circumstance. If she had ever guessed that she was going to be robbed, Margaret probably would have said that, though shaken and put out, she would manage. Because that was how she was, always able handle whatever was thrown at her. Months earlier, she had picked up and moved out of her boyfriend's apartment the morning after she overheard him making plans with another woman on the phone. Without a second thought or a glance at a map, Margaret drove north and settled in the first city with a name that she liked. She'd hoped that after a certain number of miles all of the painful memories and doubts racketing through her mind would fade, like a radio station she'd lost by driving out of range.

Leaving the town where she had lived for the last five years was like getting off at the wrong exit on a highway; she didn't know what to expect. Surviving the breakup as well as the move had proven to her that she could cope with almost anything. However, she soon realized that she had overestimated herself. In the few days since the robbery, she had barely slept. But it wasn't simply because she was afraid. The shock of her own reaction was keeping Margaret up.

She heard an engine start at the other end of the deserted parking lot and turned. Then she saw a wide, blue Buick peel out in reverse and smash into the station wagon that was parked behind her. There was a crackle and a flourish of glass from the wagon's headlight. The grille had caved in, the bumper was bent, and the front corner was a pointy snarl of metal. Margaret watched as the driver took off away from the accident, jumping the curb as they sped out of the lot. She craned over her headrest but couldn't see the person in the front seat.

They didn't even get out, she thought. *They didn't even stop.*

The one time Margaret had backed into a car, she left a note even though she hadn't made a scratch. For whoever owned the station wagon, there would be no note and, like her with the robbery, they would never know who was responsible for what happened. Margaret wasn't sure who she felt worse for.

The night she had arrived home to find her television, jewelry, and some of her furniture missing, Margaret got her first taste of a feeling that was worse than fear–uncertainty–and it felt like mud in her heart. When the police arrived, they were of little comfort or help. They basically had only two questions for her: did she have the serial numbers for any of the missing items, and could she think of anyone who could have stolen them. The answer to both was no. With that, they explained to her how unlikely it would be that they would ever find the burglar. The chances were slim.

Sometimes Margaret envisioned her furniture being set up identically somewhere else. It was almost amusing, like some sitcom-type practical joke, but not knowing who took it, who was in her apartment, was truly and profoundly unsettling. As a child, she had fallen down a flight of stairs, and the feeling was the same. One minute she was at the top of the steps, the next she was on the floor. Like her unpredictable loss of balance, the world could change without warning, and to Margaret that had always seemed unfair. Each night, her thoughts whirled uncontrollably. She couldn't look at any of her possessions without wondering if they had been touched. The question of who had done it loomed like an open door inside her mind, one that she could hear being kicked in the same way her apartment door had been. Finding the thief seemed to be the only way to close it, but what worried Margaret most was that no one ever would.

After her boyfriend Daniel had realized that she'd caught him, he said everything he could to try and make her stay. He talked continuously, pleading and explaining, and his words overwhelmed her, like a string of waves breaking on her head. She lost all of their meaning. Margaret found herself demanding details, where Daniel had taken the woman and what they had done, anything she could picture and hold on to. In the end, though, the truth–the brand of wine they drank and the spot on the couch where the other woman sat–didn't help Margaret. Those images became as vivid as her own memories, and they haunted her. It was like she'd been scraped raw, inside and out.

Margaret stared across the parking lot at the wrecked station wagon, then started her engine. The Buick hadn't gotten far up the street. She strapped on her seat belt and hit the gas.

Before she knew it, Margaret was only two cars behind the Buick and gaining. Speed blurred everything in her peripheral vision. The hot air rushing in through the windows buffeted her skin. Margaret couldn't believe what she was doing, that she was actually chasing the person. Who knew what they might do? She wouldn't let herself think that far. She ran the scene in the parking lot back to herself only to find that she'd totally forgotten about the teenager in the dumpster and why she'd been waiting for him in the first place.

After the robbery, Margaret felt as though she'd just been awakened out of a deep sleep. Every noise was shrill, excessive. The sun was too much for her eyes. She thought she could feel every thread in her clothes and the weight of air on her head. The hard, new edges of the world only made her feel more out of place. She missed her old town, if only because it was thoroughly familiar. People used to recognize her when she went to buy coffee or pick up a newspaper. Her friends were unable to make the long trip to visit, and even after a few months Margaret had barely met anyone in the new city. The move had begun to seem more like a step down than a fresh start.

One of the cars separating Margaret from the blue Buick turned onto a side street. She flashed her brights at the van in front of her, then it changed lanes, clearing the way. Margaret gunned the engine and laid on her horn for a full minute. There were other cars on the road alongside her, but she didn't bother to check if anyone was staring. She didn't care if they were.

The Buick showed no signs of slowing. Margaret tailed closely for another mile. She was anxious to see what would happen. She wanted to know what she would do. She wasn't sure. Fence posts were hurtling by, and the weeds behind them, which had been burned to blond by the sun, blurred into a yellow glow. Margaret took a deep breath and leaned into the steering wheel like she was driving through a snowstorm.

The Buick finally slowed and pulled onto the shoulder near a field. Dust rose behind its tires. The mangled, unhinged fender kept swinging after the car had come to a stop. Margaret threw her car into park, causing her wheels to grumble against the dirt. She tossed off her seat belt and sent it reeling backwards, thinking only of the faceless thief carrying her furniture away in the night.

As Margaret sprang out of her car, a series of possibilities came to her like headlines: Woman's Body Found on Side of the Road; Woman Hit by Car. Margaret knew that her thin and unimposing body probably would not match or threaten whoever was inside, so she grabbed her purse and held it in front of her as though it concealed a gun. That was all she could think of, and, like all she had done so far, it seemed somehow reasonable.

Margaret approached the Buick slowly, her footfalls audible on the gravel. When she got to the driver's window, Margaret saw a pair of hands raised in surrender. The hands belonged to a woman in her seventies with a narrow head and short, tightly permed hair. The woman's blouse hung off her bony shoulders and was tucked into a pleated skirt. She looked up at Margaret fearfully and asked, "Are you with the police?"

"No," Margaret said. "Not really."

The woman frowned, confused. "If you're not with the police, then what do you want?"

"I saw you," Margaret said. "I saw what you did."

"I don't know what this is all about, but. . . ." She let the sentence trail off, though her expression gave her away.

"Yes you do," Margaret declared. Her voice sounded odd to her, like an angry child's. "You hit that car in the parking lot, then you ran. I was there."

"I don't have to listen to this nonsense. I'm leaving."

Margaret couldn't let the woman leave. "Wait," she shouted, pretending to take hold of the imaginary gun.

The woman froze, apparently believing that she indeed had one. Margaret was unsure of what to say next, but unable to move.

The woman touched her keys and Margaret forced her hand deeper into her purse, saying, "Hey. Stop it. Take the keys out and put them on the seat."

"You're not with the police. You can't–"

Margaret pointed the imaginary gun at the woman.

"All right. All right. Please, just don't hurt me," the woman said, removing the keys from the ignition, then placing them on the passenger seat. She was afraid now. "I just don't know what all the fuss is over."

"What you did is illegal. It's against the law."

"I was going to go back."

"Then why were you going in the opposite direction?"

"Well, what are you going to do, put me under citizen's arrest?"

"No," Margaret said slowly, and the woman drew back. Then Margaret realized how menacing she sounded. That wasn't the effect she was going for, but she was too nervous to take her hand out of her purse. Her wallet was digging into her wrist, but she didn't dare shift it. Her shirt, which was already soaked through with sweat, was sticking to her skin. With the sun beating down on her, the wet material felt like a hand on her back.

"Look, I'm sorry, but I didn't mean to hit that car," the woman said. "I pushed the wrong pedal. It was a mistake. That's all."

"The wrong pedal?" Margaret couldn't believe her ears.

"I said it was an accident."

"Exactly. That's why insurance companies call it that. Has this happened before? I mean, do you choose the wrong pedal on a regular basis?"

The woman put her hand to her chest, insulted. "My Lord, no. Never. I don't drive that often."

"Do you *have* a license?"

"Yes, I do have license, thank you very much. It's just that my husband was the one who usually drove."

With that, the woman's face changed, her expression darkened. She looked tired, almost puzzled. Margaret instantly realized that the woman's husband must have died.

"But I didn't know what to do," the woman pleaded. "I saw what a mess that car was after I hit it, and I just drove away. I don't know why. I don't even know where I am now. I'm just driving, and I don't know where."

The woman was talking to Margaret, but she seemed to be speaking to herself. She gazed at the dashboard and put her fingers to her mouth, stunned by her own confession.

Margaret took her hand out of her purse. The blood that had been rushing through her body seemed to come to a full stop. She hadn't considered the possibility that the woman wouldn't know why she left until she said so, the same way Margaret couldn't conceive of being robbed until she saw the dust rings and the wear marks left on her carpet after her things had been stolen.

The road in front of them was clear, but when Margaret looked back, there was a patrol car coming toward them. The woman saw it in her rearview mirror and gasped. She turned to Margaret with plaintive eyes. There was no time for Margaret to get back into her car.

The patrol car coasted to a stop, and the officer on the passenger side rolled down his window. Margaret could feel the cool air from the air conditioner. "Flat tire?" the officer asked.

Neither Margaret nor the woman answered.

"Is there a problem, ladies?"

Margaret leaned back, putting her body in front of the crumpled corner of the woman's car. She could feel the officer following her with his eyes. The woman was silent, a stiff figure at the edge of Margaret's vision.

"No, sir," Margaret said. "I was giving this lady directions. She was lost. But I straightened her out. She knows where she's going now."

The officer studied them for a minute. Standing there between him and the woman's damaged car, it became clear to Margaret that she would never get back her chairs or her necklaces or the tiny television she had saved her money to buy. And she would never know who took them. The hazy face of the thief that she kept in her mind disappeared like a soap bubble bursting midair, then all that was left was the dull impression that she was missing something.

"All righty then," the officer said, raising his window. "You two have a good day now."

"Thank you, sir," the woman said, visibly relieved.

The patrol car pulled away, and Margaret stepped back from the Buick. As she did so, a string of cars shot past her, sending gusts of wind through her hair and clothes. She shut her eyes, but she knew that the woman was watching her, the same way she had watched the boy in the dumpster, waiting for the moment when she would be able to leave.

"I suppose I should thank you," the woman said, though she still sounded worried that Margaret would turn her in. "What are you going to do now?" she asked.

Margaret didn't answer. She kept her eyes closed and listened as the sound of the speeding cars was replaced by the low buzz of insects in a nearby field. She was going to get in her car. She was going to drive away.

For Sale
by Owner

BY MORNING, my uncle was packed and ready to move. That afternoon I got a call saying he was passed out behind the wheel of his car in the parking lot at the Shop 'n Save.

A cardboard box full of his things was sitting on a chair in the kitchen. I rested the telephone receiver on the box before I hung up, wondering what I would tell my mother. She was standing at the sink washing out a sweater. The window shades were drawn against the August heat, so the kitchen was dark, but the water that had spilled onto the counter was shining from the light that cut beneath the shades.

"If that was Ray on the phone, you should have told him to forget it," my mother said. "I told him he had to be out by five. By dinnertime. I told him that you and I had to eat dinner."

I had spent the morning mowing other people's lawns, and I was tired. I was fourteen that year, and cutting grass was my summer job. I doubted that Ray even knew how old I was or cared. He had been at our house for two days and never asked. The previous night, my mother had come home from work and found him drunk again; then she said he had to go.

"Why I let him stay in the first place, I'll never understand," she said, wringing out an arm of the sweater. I acted like I hadn't heard her. I only wanted to think simple thoughts. It was too hot for feelings.

My mother shook the water off of her hands.

"I think we have to go and get him," I said.

"Fine. Go and get him. Then tell him he has to get out."

"Aren't you coming?"

"Am I coming?" she asked, then she pulled the rubber stopper out of the sink, and I could hear the water begin to drain.

I WALKED to the Shop 'n Save and found my friend Pablo, the one who had called me, sitting on the hood of Ray's El Camino. Pablo's dirt bike was lying on the ground.

"He's not dead or anything," Pablo said.

Ray's hands were resting on the car's steering wheel, his chest rising heavily under his mesh tank top as he snored.

"Then why didn't you wake him up?" I asked.

"He's your uncle."

The window was open, so I reached in and tapped Ray's arm. He kept snoring. I took his hand and let it drop onto his knee. Still nothing.

"Beep the horn," Pablo said. The parking lot was practically empty. The only people around were the cashiers out on break. They were standing in the shade, smoking and fanning themselves with coupon circulars.

I gave the horn one long push.

With that, Ray's head snapped up, and he smashed the brake with his foot. When he realized it was just me, he dropped back into his seat, relieved.

"Jesus, man," he said, wiping the sweat from his face. "Are you trying to make me crap my pants or something?"

These were Ray's first real words to me.

"Christ, what time is it?" he asked. He slapped his cheeks, trying to wake himself up.

"Dunno," I said.

"Doesn't matter," Ray yawned. "Get in." He moved the Styrofoam cooler that was on the passenger seat to the floor.

"Are we going back home?"

"Eventually," he said.

"But I promised my mom I'd bring you back with me."

Ray reached over and opened the passenger door. "And?" he said.

Since he had arrived at our house, Ray had spent exactly ten hours there, almost all asleep. When he went out, I waited up for him, studying the few possessions he had brought: a worn tool belt, a plastic mess kit, bags of batteries and random nails, nothing truly personal. I was trying to get a sense of what he was like, but I couldn't come up with much of a picture. I was only familiar with my uncle from the stories that his name had crept into and by how it made the conversation break. My mother hardly ever talked about her brother, but when she did, she usually cut herself off midstream, like she had accidentally given away a secret. It was what she wouldn't say that made me want to know Ray even more.

Now he was leaving, and this would be my last chance to get to know him. So I walked around to the other side of the car and got in. This was how I wanted him to remember me, doing what I wanted to do, not what I was told.

Ray tilted his head and sniffed the air. "Been cutting grass?" he asked.

I nodded, surprised, and checked my shirt for stray clippings or some other evidence of what I'd done that morning.

"I can smell it," Ray said. "I've got a real sensitive nose."

He patted his pockets and dug out the car keys.

"Where are we going?" I asked.

"The Canine Carousel."

"The what? What for?"

"To get a bed."

"A dog bed?"

"No. This guy owes me. He's got one of those Craftmatic

beds. You know, the kind that moves up and down and has that Magic Fingers massage thing. We're getting that bed," Ray announced, slipping the keys into the ignition. "The guy lives over a dog groomer."

"Oh," I said.

I knew that Ray hadn't found another place to live yet and that he needed money, that other times he'd lived at the YMCA or in his car, taking showers at the beach and following the illegal immigrants around to the orange farms to pick for under-the-table wages. But I hadn't heard any of those things from him.

His first night at our house, he had sacked out on a cot in my room without a word. I stayed up for an hour listening to him breathe in his sleep. The next day, he was gone before breakfast and didn't come home until after midnight. I hung around, hoping to run into him, but he never showed. The only time I'd even heard Ray speak was when I was still half-asleep. It was near dawn, and I could hear him through my bedroom wall as he talked on the telephone in the kitchen. I overheard him tell somebody to "shove it." Later, I found myself saying the same thing under my breath to an elderly man who'd scolded me for missing a patch of grass in his backyard.

"Okay, let's roll," Ray said.

"Wait. What about Pablo?"

He was sitting on the ground next to his dirtbike, flicking pebbles across the parking lot and waiting for me to invite him with us.

"What about him?"

"Can he come too?"

"Hmm. I don't know. He looks kinda retarded."

"He's not. He just looks like that."

In the harsh sunlight, Pablo's face was heavy and flat and big in a way that didn't match his boyish frame. It was as if he'd only gotten older from the neck up. On top of that, his hair was all uneven, like he'd cut it himself with a pair of school scissors, and that gave him a scrappy look. "His cat has seizures," I explained in Pablo's defense, "and one time he took some of its pills to see what would happen. But he did the math to find out how many he'd have to take for his weight compared to his cat's."

It was a stupid thing to say, but that was all that came to mind. In the end, though, it didn't seem to matter. "Fine," Ray relented. "He can come."

I shouted to Pablo to put his dirt bike in the back and jump in. Then the three of us crammed into the front seat and Pablo seemed happy, like whatever we were going to do would be a good thing because we'd be doing it together.

"Where're we going?" Pablo asked.

"The Canine Carousel," I told him.

"Cool."

Ray started the car, then it died. He tried again. This time the engine choked and wheezed, then it caught. Ray crossed himself in thanks.

As we coasted through the lanes of the parking lot, something popped under the tires. Pablo and I waited for Ray to stop, but he didn't. We were riding over glass, but Ray kept going, probably out of fear that the car might not start again.

We drove around on the freeway for what felt like an hour. I could feel every pothole and every change in the surface of the road because the car sat so low to the ground. Other cars would pass us, and the music playing inside would blare and then fade. There was no radio in Ray's El Camino; it had been torn out. I couldn't tell if the thing had been stolen or if Ray had ripped it out to pawn it for cash. Either was equally possible.

"You see that mill over there?" Ray said, motioning to an enormous box of a building that hunkered on the side of the highway. "They make cereal there. You're supposed to be able to smell it. Like when they're making bran flakes or whatever, the air smells like bran flakes." He lifted his head, closing his eyes, and breathed in deeply. "But it doesn't smell like anything today, does it?"

"That sucks," Pablo said, shaking his head, genuinely disappointed.

We got off the freeway and onto a street lined with cement-block houses, each with its own rutted collar of dirt. After the houses stopped coming, there were only traffic lights and Cyclone fences and a ragged line of cypress trees. We were on some desolate back road, and I was thinking that the Canine Carousel had to be the sort of place that people only found by accident. Then Ray pointed it out.

It was an old house overrun by weeds that stood alone in the middle of nowhere. The porch, which was the storefront, had been painted pink, and a wooden dog bone hung in the window. Birds had made nests in the O and the U of the word *Carousel* on the store's sign. The whole place looked deserted.

Ray circled the building and parked in the back by a flight of stairs that led to the second floor.

"Is anybody home?" I asked.

"Not yet," Ray answered. "But soon, probably."

He cased the rear of the house. The window next to the back door was open a few inches. Without hesitation, he forced it up.

"Up and at 'em," Ray hollered.

I got out of the car reluctantly. Pablo slid out after me. "What about the guy? The guy who owes you?" I asked.

"What about him?" Ray bent down, poised to hoist me through the window.

The reality that I was about to break into somebody's house finally got to me. My mouth dried up, my stomach seemed to be full of wet cement. The sudden thought of my mother waiting at home sent a surge of doubt right through me, but I told myself to ignore it. Ray was waiting, and I felt lame just standing there.

The windowsill was as high as my shoulders, and I held it as I balanced on Ray's hand and thigh. I glanced back at Pablo. He gave me the thumbs up. Ray lifted me to the window, squeezing my shoes hard, then one of my ankles, and it seemed like I couldn't shake him loose if I tried. As I crawled inside the house, I accidentally knocked a plant off a table. The pot clattered to the floor.

"Quiet," Ray said. "This isn't a parade."

"Sorry," I whispered.

In the dim light, it appeared as if I was in an empty kitchen. Metal tables and tubs lined the walls. Spray nozzles hung in loops from the ceiling. The thick, sweet smell of pet shampoo permeated the room.

Ray knocked on the back door. When I opened it, he pushed past me. He was scoping out the room to make sure the coast was clear; then the scent of the shampoo must have hit him. He looked upset, almost offended. "Damn," he huffed. "That smell could give you whiplash."

I didn't know what to say to that, so I asked him where Pablo was instead.

"On duty."

Ray led me upstairs to a hallway that had two doors. Two apartments, I assumed.

"Which one?" I asked.

"Hell if I know."

He tried the handle on the door to the left and, to my surprise and his, it opened. Ray peered in, then gestured for me to follow.

The room was paneled, and there was a painting of a moose by a lake on the wall. All of the furniture seemed to have been stolen from a motel except the bed, which sat, bent at an angle, in front of a television that had a few links of cut chain fastened to it.

Piles of old newspapers and magazines littered the room. The dust on the dresser had matted into balls. There was so much junk lying around that I could barely see the floor.

Ray stepped over a heap of clothes and picked up the bed's control box. He raised the foot of the bed, then lowered it, playing with the settings like a kid with a new toy. Watching him, I felt like a visitor, like someone who had come to check out an apartment while the owner wasn't home. I felt chosen too, to be where I wasn't supposed to be.

"Now who wouldn't want to buy a bed like this?" Ray asked proudly. "This is top-of-the-line comfort. People would kill for comfort like this. Am I right?"

He patted the bed, then started stripping it.

"Don't you want the sheets?"

"Nah. They look a little ripe."

They looked fine to me. Nothing a spin in the washer wouldn't take care of. "You might as well," I said. "If you're taking the bed, take all of it."

Ray's brow furrowed. "Let me tell you something about these sheets," he said. He held them up to his nose. "They have never been washed. I can smell it. Never. I'm no expert, but these babies are in a bad way. They stink."

He bunched the bedclothes up in his hand and smelled them all over. "I wouldn't try and sell these to anybody. They'd think I was crazy."

And they might be right, I thought.

Ray threw the sheets on the floor. Lying there, they looked like cartoon ghosts. Then they began to blend in with the rest of the garbage. I thought the man might not even notice them amid the mess. In my mind, I pictured him as short and angry, with a life as small as his single room full of stolen furniture. I couldn't envision Ray living in a room like this one, but then again, he didn't have a place to live, period.

My mother had told me that Ray always claimed he was going to buy a Jacuzzi when he got an apartment of his own. He said he would even sleep in it and that he'd get a little inner tube to put around his neck so that he wouldn't drown. According to her, Ray saw life out of the corner of his eye, where only the thing that was farthest away was clear. As I stood beside him in that cluttered apartment, I decided it was too bad that Ray's sense of sight wasn't as good as his sense of smell, and I wondered if anything would ever be right in front of him.

He pulled the bed away from the wall to unplug it and discovered a tangle of electric cords, which he started yanking. I crouched to help him. The sound of a car passing by outside made both of us freeze. We held our breath until the noise drifted down to nothing.

"You like mowing lawns?" Ray asked. I thought he must have smelled the grass on me again.

"It's not so bad," I said. But really, I didn't like it. It was an easy thing to do, but being responsible for other people's lawns made me uneasy. I found myself dreading the job, getting uptight about how well I did it. There was a light but disturbing weight that came with taking care of something that was not my own, and I hated to think that that feeling was just a hint of what the future held.

"It's only one summer," I told him. When I looked up from the mound of cords, Ray was listening intently, as though this was the only thing he needed to know from me, and that was why we hadn't spoken before.

"That's good," he said. "It's good to like your job."

I couldn't read his voice, but I instantly wanted to take back what I had said. The words, now spoken, seemed pinned to me, like I had agreed to something without knowing it. But it was too late.

Ray slipped the bed's cord free and began twirling it with a smile. "Now we're in business," he said, his grin flashing behind the spinning cord.

BY THE TIME we'd gotten the top mattress down the back stairs, the sun had moved. Shadows were growing out of the high weeds, darkening the crumbling asphalt lot. The image of my mother standing at the front door flared in my mind, and again I shoved it away.

"Keep up the good work," Ray shouted to Pablo, who was

at his post, sitting near the edge of the building; he was on guard watching the street. Pablo saluted him crisply like a cadet. He seemed glad just to be a part of the whole thing. I knew how he felt.

"Come on," Ray ordered, hustling me up the steps. "We're not done yet."

We went back into the apartment and cleared a path through the junk so that we could move out the bottom part of the bed. The box spring was heavy from the motor inside, and it felt like it weighed a ton. Ray told me to wait in the hall while he pushed it closer to the door.

The hallway was only slightly larger than the bed, and it was dark. It was going be difficult to maneuver in. I paced the length of it, then a voice behind me said, "I see you."

I jerked my head toward the sound. A little girl was peeking out from behind the door to the other apartment.

"I see you," she repeated.

The chain lock was still on, and she was pressing her face between the door and the jamb. All that I could make out was one of her eyes, the swell of a cheek, and the flat run of her torso and leg. She was wearing a woman's slip that brushed the floor because she was so small—too small, I realized, to be able to reach the chain. Which meant that either she had stood on a chair to lock it or somebody else was home.

My heart started to drum in my chest. I could hear Ray moving the bed in the man's apartment. The wheels were making a noise like desperate crying, then the sound stopped short. The bed must have gotten stuck on something.

Voice low, I asked, "What did you see?"

"That's not your house."

I was trying to get a view into her apartment to see if she was alone.

"I might tell on you," she whispered. I didn't know if she was mimicking me or if she was doing it because whoever was inside was asleep. "But I might not," she added. Her fingers were wrapped around the door, pulling it to her as far as it would go on the chain. "But I could," she said.

Ray called out to me to help him, and she watched my face. I was debating whether I should tell Ray about her; then it occurred to me that, honestly, I had no idea what he would do.

"Are you deaf?" Ray shouted. I spun around. He was standing in the doorway, panting and sweating from exertion. I turned back to the other door. To my relief, it was closed.

"I'm not getting any younger here," Ray said, snapping his fingers.

We spent the next fifteen minutes shoving and muscling the bottom part of the bed through the hallway. I kept my eye on the other door the whole time, but it never opened. I started to wonder if I'd dreamed what had happened, if the little girl was just a figment of my imagination. Part of me was hoping she was.

When we reached the back staircase, Ray yelled to Pablo. "Come on this side with me," he said to him. "Hurry up."

Pablo scurried over to his assigned position and took a corner of the bed. I was at the top of the stairs, balancing the other end.

"Okay, men. Ready?"

Together the three of us steadied the heavy bed frame and prepared to do the entire flight in one shot. But a few steps into it, Ray got ahead of Pablo and lost his grip.

The bed fell from my hands, tumbling past Ray and pushing Pablo with it down the steps. He hit the railing, then the ground. I only heard myself cry out afterwards, like an echo.

When it was over, Pablo was sprawled across the dirt and the bed was lying awkwardly along the stairs, blocking the way. I hopped over it and ran to Pablo's side. Ray ambled down after me and stooped over Pablo's body.

"Well this isn't good," he said, scratching his face thoughtfully.

"You let go," I shouted. As I knelt over Pablo, my shadow

was thrown across his face. His expression, normally blank and thick, had become knowingly peaceful.

"He's down for the count. That's for sure."

I held my hand over Pablo's mouth. Thankfully, he was breathing.

"This is your fault," I yelled. "He wasn't even supposed to be helping."

"He's your friend," Ray said. "I didn't say he had to come."

I was still on my knees, so my eyes were level with Ray's stomach. From the way his mesh tank top hung on his body, it seemed like I could see right through him. In a single motion, I leapt up and lunged at him, driving my fingers at his neck.

Ray caught me and pushed me back onto the steps. He held me in a hard gaze and waved his finger in one slow swipe, carving the air between us.

"Don't," he said.

Then Pablo drew in a sharp breath and opened his eyes. He began to cough and blink, confused, shocked. I scrambled back over to him and helped him sit up.

"Are you okay? Are you okay?" I must have asked him a hundred times.

Pablo nodded and rubbed his head, still stunned.

"See. Just got the wind knocked out of him is all," Ray said, clapping his hands together. "Glad to have you back, Pablo. Now let's get this mattress into the car."

"Don't you think we should go to the doctor or something?"

"Nah. He'll live. We'll lay him on top of the bed for the ride home. It's a bed, isn't it?"

I couldn't say anything. Neither my brain nor my mouth was willing to work.

"And as long as I don't have to slam on the brakes, he'll be fine back there. Don't worry. I'll drive like a nun. Now give me a hand. This thing is heavy."

We laid Pablo out on the mattress, and Ray tied the bed's cord over his chest. "This is one comfortable bed, am I right?"

Pablo shook his head weakly, then Ray patted the bed and

told me to hop in. When we were both inside, he opened the cooler and wiped his face with the melted ice, offering it to me when he was done. I hesitated, then did the same. The water felt like the coldest, cleanest thing I'd ever touched.

Ray drove home a different way than we had come. Now all of the houses we drove by were long and low, each set at the back end of a manicured piece of property. When we passed a house with a white car parked out on its lawn, Ray stopped. He cruised back in reverse until we were right beside the car, a pristine Caddie convertible with a sign that read For Sale by Owner clipped under one of the windshield wipers. A pair of ceramic deer was standing in front of the car like they were caught in its headlights.

"Be right back," Ray said.

After a quick glance around, he jogged over to the car and plucked the sign out from under the wiper blade. I had to look away. I could see a sliver of Pablo's arm in the side mirror. I imagined the wind picking it up, lifting it, and fluttering Pablo's fingers. The vision disappeared, and I felt sick and exhausted. It seemed as if the sun could shine right through me, like a flashlight through a fingertip. Maybe the girl was real and she would tell on us, I thought. I wasn't sure if that would be bad thing. I turned back and studied the lawn where the white car was parked. The grass was neat, and a checkerboard pattern had been cut into it. I could do the pattern, but I didn't think I could have done it that well.

Ray put the sign in the back with Pablo and his dirt bike and the bed, then we drove away casually. "Don't want to look too conspicuous," he said.

On the way home, we pulled off the freeway into a truck stop.

"It's late," Ray said, and he was right. By then, he and his boxes should have been long gone. "I'm gonna call your mom," he announced, "but I think you better talk to her. You know. She'll listen to you."

Ray went inside the truck stop. The pay phone was by a

picture window, and I could see him pick up the receiver and fix his hair in the silver reflection on the phone's front panel. I could see his mouth moving. Then he was waving me in, motioning for me to come and talk to my mother. Behind him, a lit pie case was spinning slowly. It was as though I was watching television with the volume off and, in that absence of sound, I could hear all of the things I should have said, as well as the things I knew I wouldn't.

Ray knocked on the picture window impatiently, then pressed his hand to the glass. For a moment, that was all I could see of him.

The High Month

ADRIENNE BROKE INTO Richard's car with a wire hanger, then she drove until the car was out of gas.

The tank ran dry near a highway on-ramp, about a hundred yards from a bar appropriately named the End of the Road Watering Hole. On the bar's roof stood a wooden cutout of a cowboy on a rearing horse that was silhouetted against the white December sky. Crested by the cowboy's lasso, the listing building was so glum and tacky it was almost comic. Of all places, Adrienne found it fitting she would end up there.

Richard had given her a key to his apartment—a gesture he said proved how serious he was about their relationship—and Adrienne knew where he kept a spare for the ignition, so jimmying the door to his vintage Mustang was the only part of her plan that had involved any real risk or effort. After she had gotten the button lock up, she let her guard down and took off. When the Mustang coasted to a stop, Adrienne realized that the lesson she had been trying to teach Richard about priorities—namely obsessing over his car—would not be nearly as apparent to him as the one she had just learned about keeping her eye on the gas gauge. The irony wasn't lost on her.

Adrienne folded the hanger into her purse and locked the doors, then left the car in the ditch where it had stalled and headed for the End of the Road.

Upon entering the bar, a voice called out to her, "Is it raining?"

Adrienne could make out a few dark forms in cowboy hats sitting on stools, and there was a couple in a booth by the door, but because she was looking into the shadowy room with daylight behind her, Adrienne wasn't sure exactly where the question had come from.

"No," she said tentatively.

"As long as it's not raining, I'll be happy," the voice announced. "It shouldn't rain on Christmas. That'd be just plain wrong."

Once inside, Adrienne could tell that it was the bartender who had spoken. He was a hefty, solid man, and he wore a bandanna around his forehead. He was leaning into the bar like he was the only thing holding it up.

"Is there a service station around here?" Adrienne asked. "I ran out of gas up the road."

"Afraid not," the bartender said, shaking his head sympathetically. "Next one's up the highway a good five miles."

There was no way she could walk that distance. And none of the other men at the bar were jumping up to offer her a ride. Though all were squarely in their sixties and seemingly benign, Adrienne doubted whether she would have gone even if they had offered.

"Maybe you could call somebody to come and get you," the bartender suggested.

Adrienne wished it were that easy. She had called in sick that morning to the insurance company where she worked, so she couldn't phone anybody there for help. And if she called a friend, then she'd have to tell them just what she had been up to. Adrienne's only other option was to call Richard. He was an accountant, a serious yet thoughtful man who, like any of his spreadsheets, looked good on paper. He was loving, had a steady job, his own home, and most of his hair. To Adrienne, who at thirty-eight was already once divorced, Richard was a real catch. However, this stunt she'd pulled with the car would likely scare him straight off the line.

"Nobody to call," Adrienne said, answering the bartender. An empty tank had not been part of her scheme. She slumped down on a stool to think.

The syrupy twang of a country ballad filled the bar, which, Adrienne judged, had probably been a barn in a previous incarnation. The place still had the drafty feel of a building not meant to be lived in. All of the wall studs were exposed, and the light fixtures hung from sagging rafters alongside alternating rows of spurs and branding irons, the only visible nod to a cowboy theme besides the cutout on the roof. Strands of colored Christmas lights strung around support beams did little to brighten the decor or the room itself, which was so dimly lit that Adrienne found she could no longer see the couple by the door from where she sat. When she squinted, all she could discern was a poster at the end of the bar bearing a photograph of a wrecked pickup truck surrounded by cartoon sprigs of holly. The poster read: "Don't take the *Merry* out of Merry Christmas."

"We have drink specials," the bartender offered. "Half-price shots for ladies. That's not supposed to start until seven, but I'd make an exception."

Adrienne attempted a smile. "It's a little too early for me."

"Suit yourself," he said. "But the offer stands."

He went back to watching the television that was mounted on the wall. A weatherman was tracing a path of storm clouds that was moving up the Southern coast. The satellite showed a staticky haze whirling its way toward the ocean, hiding brown stretches of land all over the state. Adrienne tried to focus on what to do about the car but, like the land on-screen, any ideas were quickly swept over by indecision.

Adrienne had been with Richard when he purchased the midnight blue, '69 Mustang a month earlier. It was a present to himself. "I know midlife crises are really eighties," Richard said, "but this car makes me feel good." Adrienne had to admit that it was a handsome automobile, practically a work of art. It sat low to the ground and looked razor sharp. But there was one problem. Richard's answer to his midlife crisis had quickly turned into Adrienne's current predicament.

In the beginning, she could overlook it when he would scold her for shutting the car door too roughly or pulling the seat belt too hard. She had been willing to put up with it because when they weren't actually in the car, Richard turned all of his attention over to her, acting as if she were a delicate flower he'd been given to hold. No other man had ever treated her that well. They saw each other every day, and Richard wouldn't take no for an answer when it came to wining and dining her. For Adrienne, it was as though she had her own spotlight, like a jewel in a museum case, and she had gotten accustomed to it. Richard was a sweet, gentle man, quick to give his heart, but Adrienne soon discovered that it was possible to go beyond love. And that was what he had done. Only not with her.

"Hey, it's okay," the bartender said to Adrienne. She knew she must have looked upset. He probably thought she was going to cry. "It's only an empty gas tank," he declared. "It's not like your car blew up."

Adrienne had to laugh. The bartender was right. The car wasn't gone. It just wasn't where it was supposed to be.

She had planned to move the Mustang while Richard was at work, to park it around the block from his apartment and wait for him to return. When he came home, he would immediately notice that the car was missing, but before he could get too worked up, Adrienne would step in and explain everything in the hope that he might realize just how ridiculous he was behaving about his car.

Once Adrienne was on the road, however, she found it difficult to turn back. She had never been behind the Mustang's wheel, and hitting the gas felt like an overdue snub. Each night before Richard would get into bed with her, he would check on the car from the window. He washed it every week by hand.

He still doted on her, but Adrienne didn't like sharing the spotlight. She had daydreams of taking a sledgehammer to the car's hood, a chainsaw, a container of lighter fluid—wild visions. In the end, that was why she thought her trick would work. If Richard wasn't so preoccupied with the Mustang, then she wouldn't have to be either. It hadn't dawned on Adrienne that *anybody* would be upset to find their car missing, not until it was too late.

As she sat at the bar tracing the nicks in the shellac, Adrienne tried to predict what Richard would do when he found out what she had done. Realistically, he would break up with her. She didn't want to think about it.

Adrienne forced herself up. "Ladies room?" she asked. The bartender poked his thumb toward the rear of the building. She pushed in her stool and headed toward the back, then something moved at the edge of her vision, and Adrienne stopped short.

There was a man sitting at a table in the far corner of the room. She hadn't noticed him before. He was watching her.

"Excuse me, miss," he said in a mellow drawl. "Mind if I ask you something?"

The man was dressed in a Santa suit. His beard and cap lay on the table beside several empty bottles of beer. Two of the buttons on his red jacket were open, exposing the pillow that was stuffed inside. Adrienne couldn't understand how she had missed him, but the dim, old barn did offer plenty of room to hide in. That may have been the very reason he was there.

"I know you don't know me," the man intoned. "But I'd like to ask you for a favor." He cheerfully motioned for Adrienne to join him.

His scalp was gleaming and he needed a shave, but he had a wide, ingratiating smile. He was, she guessed, no younger than fifty. He was probably also drunk, but Adrienne's instincts told her that he was harmless. Anyway, if he tried anything, she felt sure she could get to one of the empty beer bottles before he could get to her.

"Come on," the man said. "I didn't ask you to sit on my lap. That's not the favor. What I want is of a purely innocent nature."

"I have Mace," Adrienne lied.

"And I value my eyesight."

"So what's the favor?"

He pushed a chair toward her with his foot. Adrienne took a seat cautiously, keeping her distance. The man shoved up the furry cuffs of his coat and put out his hand, which Adrienne shook quickly. He said his name was Bruce.

"My job," Bruce began, gesturing to his suit, "is complicated. To say the least."

Bruce spoke with such intensity that Adrienne had to reconsider exactly what was involved in playing Santa. Bouncing children on your knee and listening to their Christmas lists didn't sound all that complex. Bruce must have read the doubt on her face. "What? You don't believe me?"

"No. Really, I do," she told him. No need to get the man riled up, Adrienne thought.

"Well, I guess I should say my job *was* complicated. I was fired," Bruce said, taking a swig from his beer. "Thank Christ."

Then came a strained silence. Adrienne examined the floor.

"It wasn't a good job. It was worse than I expected. But what isn't?" he added. "I had children asking for Ferraris and a million dollars, which is typical. I also had two kids ask if they could have their schools burned down before the end of the holiday break. And one who wanted to know if he could have his stepfather killed. Literally killed." Bruce rubbed the corners of his mouth. He looked as though he was having trouble forming his next sentence. Adrienne was beginning to regret her decision to sit down.

"After that," he went on, "I started telling kids they could wish for whatever they wanted, but that it didn't mean they were going to get it. In fact, I said, the odds weren't good. The mothers did not appreciate this, of course. Neither did my boss." The cuffs of Bruce's coat slid back down his arms. "I know I'm not the first Santa to feel like this, to have this reaction. I know this isn't an original complaint. But let me ask you something," he said, locking Adrienne in a soulful stare. "How can I be Santa *and* be a moral guy?"

Bruce let the question hang between them, acting as though he hadn't asked it and rolling the bottom of a beer bottle over the wet ring it had left on the table. Then, to Adrienne's astonishment, he began to unbutton the top of his pants.

"Wait," she cried, reaching for one of the bottles.

In a single swift motion, Bruce ripped the pillow from under his pants and shirt and threw it to the floor. Relieved, Adrienne fell back into her chair.

"What a terrible job," Bruce stated flatly.

Outside, drops of rain began to hit the windows. From what Adrienne had heard on the television a few minutes ago, it was going to rain on Christmas. The weatherman had put up his hands defeatedly and wagged his finger at the swirling clouds. The forecast made no difference to Adrienne. Whatever the weather, she rarely looked forward to the holidays. Like trying to decorate a palm tree instead of a pine, Christmas was always especially difficult and unsatisfying and, in the end, it only reminded her of what she didn't have to celebrate. This year, it seemed things would be no different.

Bruce eyed the television. The volume had been turned up, and the bartender was flipping channels. It seemed as though Christmas music was playing on every station. Adrienne decided to give Bruce another minute to ask his favor, then she was determined to excuse herself. She thought about calling Richard, but still hadn't come up with a way to explain herself. Each minute that passed was more time that he had to agonize over his missing Mustang. She was making the situation worse simply by sitting there.

"Just look at him," Bruce said.

Adrienne thought he meant someone on television.

"Who does he think he is? It's not like this is the Ritz. It's only some dirty, old honky-tonk bar." Bruce wore a wounded expression but sounded angry.

Adrienne followed his line of sight straight to the bartender's back, and finally she understood. She was surprised that she hadn't figured it out sooner. The bartender must have cut Bruce off, and the favor he was going to ask was that she buy a round of beer for him. It was as if he was trying to work off a stubborn soberness, but because Bruce wasn't acting totally bombed, Adrienne wondered why he didn't just go to another bar. Then she remembered shifting the Mustang into drive, what little effort it took to lose herself in the lull of the motor. Getting caught up in something was the easy part.

"That man doesn't have the giving spirit," Bruce hinted.

"Another one of these?" She pointed to the label on one of the bottles.

"You read my mind," he said, grinning.

Adrienne went up to the bar and ordered. The bartender glanced in Bruce's direction. "This for you?" he asked.

She wasn't expecting the question, so she hemmed and hawed and took too long to answer.

"Sorry," the bartender said. "I already told that guy enough is enough."

When Adrienne returned to the table empty-handed, Bruce was grave. She thought he might leap up and sweep all of the bottles onto the floor. It was possible, though unlikely. When Bruce wasn't smiling, the deep creases in his face gave him a harsh, ravaged look, something the fake beard must have covered, but his body didn't appear as if it would cooperate for such a feat of exuberance.

"It's all right. It's not your fault," Bruce said, beckoning for her to sit back down.

"Look, I should be going," Adrienne said, a little louder than she'd intended.

"Where are you going to go? You don't have any gas." Bruce nodded toward the bar, indicating that he had heard her talking before. He wasn't threatening her, merely pointing out what she'd let herself temporarily forget. Once reminded, Adrienne could picture the empty tank turning into a vast cavern. She imagined an eerie wind whistling through its darkness, her mind manifesting stress in cartoonish horror.

"So where could you go?" Bruce asked.

"Nowhere, I guess."

Now Adrienne sounded as bitter as Bruce did. She didn't like her choices: calling Richard over for a confrontation she wasn't prepared for or walking out in the rain in search of a gas station. Neither was appealing, and both would speed up the inevitable.

The rain had picked up. Adrienne found herself listening to its rhythm on the roof as though it was a favorite piece of music. She waited, anticipating a break like the end of a song that would signal her to move, to do something about the gas. The interruption came instead from Bruce saying, "How far away is your car?"

"Does it matter?"

"How far?"

"Just down the road. Why?"

Bruce grabbed the pillow off the floor and stood up. "Let's go."

"Where?"

"Parking lot," he said. Hesitant, Adrienne remained. "Come on," Bruce said, waving her along. He was halfway across the room. After a few seconds, Adrienne acquiesced.

They stepped outside and stood under the overhang for a minute. The sky, heavy and gray as iron, seemed to be only a few feet overhead. Rain was streaming down, filling the potholes in the bar's lot.

"Now what?" Adrienne asked. She was willing to follow Bruce out of the bar, but not much farther.

"Wait here a minute," he said.

Bruce ambled across the lot to a beat-up sedan and opened the trunk with a key. After tossing the pillow inside, he pulled out a gas can and a piece of tubing, then held them up for her to see. "You need gas, right?"

He went over to the car parked in the space marked Reserved for Staff next to the building and removed the gas cap. "Come and hold this can," Bruce said. Adrienne did as he asked.

"Are you really that pissed off at the bartender that you

would steal the gas right out of his tank?" She huddled her shoulders and cupped one hand over her eyes. The rain made her feel like she had to shout to be heard.

"One good turn deserves another, don't you think?" Bruce picked up the tube and stretched it out so it would reach his mouth. "How badly do you want this gas anyway, huh?"

Adrienne thought about all the time she had already wasted and moved the can into place by the end of the tube.

"Have you ever done this before?" she asked.

"No, but I know how to do it. And I've tasted gasoline before, so I think I'm prepared."

"Somebody else cut you off and you got desperate?"

"Funny," Bruce said, glowering. "I used to be a fireman. But I lost that job too. Guess red really isn't my color."

Bruce took a few deep breaths, put the tube to his lips, then inhaled one long drag. The gasoline came coursing out of the tank and he dropped the tube into the can, spitting and choking on the mouthful of gasoline he'd gotten. Adrienne searched for a spigot somewhere on the building. Unable to locate one, she gave Bruce a napkin from her purse. He wiped his tongue with it, gagging.

"So they make you drink gasoline before you fight fires?" Adrienne asked as the can began to fill. She felt like talking, an anxious response to her impending meeting with Richard.

"No," Bruce said with a cough. "That was an accident, a mistake during a demonstration. One of many."

The gasoline was pulsing through the rain-spattered tube, causing the can to rock in the mud. Bruce brushed down the sleeves of the Santa suit and patted out the rainwater.

"This is a pretty good coat. Doubt if I could wear it that often, but at least I didn't have to pay for it."

"Do you still have your fireman's outfit?"

"I had to turn it in."

"That's too bad."

"The whole thing was too bad," he said, checking the can. "I'd just washed it."

Bruce wiped the rain from his face. "Jeez, that was ten years ago," he said, remembering. "It was August, and I'd been hanging my uniform up to dry when I heard a call come in over the police band radio. A man had jumped off a bridge. The police were trying to find his body in the river."

Adrienne was taken aback. She wasn't sure what to say or if she should say anything at all. Bruce looked around and over his shoulder like the memory was coming up on him from behind.

"My house was right on the bank of that river," Bruce said. "I knew where the cops were looking. And I knew they were up too high. I could tell that the current would've swept the body much farther downstream. I had a little motor boat back then, and I took a sheet and a net and went out on the water." Bruce bent down and shook the tube to encourage the gasoline to flow. "I didn't really think about what I was doing. I was already on probation for not showing up and for screwing around, and I was trying to make right. Redeem myself, I suppose. Show everybody that I wasn't the guy they thought I was."

Bruce held the tube as the last bit of gasoline filled the can, then pulled it from the tank. After a moment, he said, "I found the body and brought it to shore. It was like it was right there waiting for me. But when I called in, they told me I'd broken procedure in a big way. A day later, I was out. I had to bring all of the gear back to the station or else they'd fine me. The uniform was still wet from when I'd washed it."

"But you found the body," Adrienne said.

"That's right." Bruce took the tube back to his trunk. "And they were dragging bodies out of that river for weeks after that. August is what cops call a 'high month.' There are others, but really, it's any month where people start acting crazy or, more to the point, when a lot of people die. December's one because of the holidays and all. In August, though, it's the heat. It changes people. They either lose their minds wanting to be cool, wanting it so badly, or they drown trying to get cool." Bruce slammed his trunk. He walked back over to Adrienne and looked at her squarely, thick drops of rain pelting his face. "Maybe after all those bodies went missing, they were sorry they fired me."

"Maybe," Adrienne replied.

Rainwater was getting into the gas can. Bruce put the lid on it. "We don't want any rain getting in our perfectly good gas," he said.

The humming sound of traffic on the nearby highway made it seem as though the air was quivering, being split by the rain. Adrienne thought she could feel the motion on her skin.

"You did me a favor, well, tried to, so now I did you one," Bruce said, hoisting the can up onto his knee. "Go on," he told her. "You can go home now."

"What about the gas can? It's yours."

"Keep it," he said, staring out at the puddles that had collected on the lot.

Bruce passed Adrienne the hefty container, which she had to hold with both hands, then he went over to the side of the building to stand under the overhang. Adrienne trailed him.

"But isn't there something else I can do for you? Give you a ride or something?" She was biding time. She wasn't ready to face Richard.

"Nah. You've done your good deed for the day."

The rain was coming down hard now. The grass at the edge of the lot shuddered under the torrent.

"You're going to have to make a run for it," Bruce said. "Do you think you can make it?"

Adrienne felt herself nod yes, though she wasn't sure just how she would make it, not in any sense. She lifted the can into her arms and let it press its weight into her wet shirt. As it fell, the rain sounded like clapping hands, an audience after the curtain had closed. Adrienne thought about the pale leather seats in Richard's car, how the water would stain them and how her body would leave a shadow of itself there, maybe permanently. That was the image she clenched in her mind as she stepped out from under the overhang into the downpour.

Edith Drogan's Uncle Is Dead

THE DAY AFTER I lost my job, my mother called and asked me to come over and put up some wallpaper. In the weeks since I'd moved back to town, I hadn't visited home once. My excuse had been that I still needed time to get settled in the room I'd taken at a boardinghouse near the city limits. The truth was I thought I'd be more comfortable on the ledge of a building than in the house where I grew up.

This time when my mother phoned, she didn't give me the chance to refuse. She had found something under the old wallpaper while she was taking it down, a message written on the wall. It made her uncomfortable, she said, and she wanted me to get rid of it, cover it back up. No excuses.

At the time, I didn't have a car. I would've walked, but outside a cold rain was barreling through the gutters, turning the patch of yard in front of the boardinghouse to mud. What I needed was a ride. But my mother had already left, said she couldn't stay in the house with that stuff on the wall and that she wouldn't come back until it was gone. The only other person I knew who had a car was a guy named Loames who stayed in a room on the third floor of the boardinghouse. I hadn't met him yet, but I'd heard about him. Loames was known to keep to himself and to never flush the toilet. Considering my options, I was willing to overlook a few questionable characteristics. So I went to Loames's room and knocked. A voice inside simply replied, "Enter."

When I opened the door, Loames was sitting on the edge of his tightly made bed, a magazine in his lap. I guessed that he was in his forties, but it was hard to tell for sure. He had bad skin, and his dark, coarse hair was packed down with gel. He looked like an extra from an old gangster movie, the type that didn't make it to the end of the film. Loames stared right at me, but didn't say a word. Not the greeting I'd been hoping for.

"Listen," I said, clearing my throat. "I know you don't know me, but I need to get to my mother's house across town, and I don't have a car. With this weather, I could use a lift. I can't pay you, but I could probably get you some coffee or maybe something to eat in exchange for the ride."

"You going there for dinner?" Loames asked, closing his magazine. He had a surprisingly mild voice. "It's a little early for dinner."

"No. I have to put up some wallpaper."

"Sounds like a two-man job."

I thought it over. I could use the help, but Loames had a look on his face that I couldn't read. Since I'd moved into the boardinghouse, I'd never seen anybody talk to the guy. The house, a converted Baptist church, had a painting of Jesus and a rainbow on the living room wall, and the only time I'd ever seen Loames was when he was sitting in there alone, reading *National Geographics* by the light that was positioned in the ceiling to illuminate Jesus' head. Now, even though a boardinghouse isn't the sort of place where people come to buddy up and make friends, I figured there had to be a reason everyone stayed away from Loames. Then again, maybe he was just a loner. I could understand that. I could even relate.

"Sure," I said finally. "I guess I could use a hand."

"Good. You and me, we'll get it done."

"You know I can't give you any money, right?"

"I know," Loames said. "When're we leaving?"

I WAITED on the front porch until Loames pulled up in a weathered station wagon with wood paneling on the sides. Once I'd gotten into the car, I realized that the windshield was almost opaque with condensation. Loames drove on in spite of the haze. "Can you see?" I asked him.

"Enough," Loames nodded. "Anyway, I've been here so long I could drive any of these roads with my eyes closed."

"But you don't know where I live."

"Yeah, but I bet I could find it."

I gave Loames directions to my house, then we rode the rest of the way in silence. When we parked, Loames hit the curb.

"Is your mother going to mind about me coming along?" he asked.

"No. Anyway, she's out playing bingo at the rectory. The tenant she's got is probably here, though. He stays upstairs."

Loames switched off the engine. "If she's got a room, why don't you live there?"

Explaining to this man, a stranger, why I had avoided my own house for the past fourteen years was the last thing I wanted to do. The only reason I had moved back to town was because I felt sure I could get a job there, either on the city docks or at one of the service stations. And I did. I started working part-time as a mechanic at an auto body shop until I was let go for lack of business. Seemed my luck had been nothing but bad for awhile, and I had gotten used to it the way you get used to a pair of shoes being too tight: it pinches, but it's the same kind of pain over and over. A month earlier, my girlfriend had left me and taken almost everything we owned, including our Mazda. A week later, my landlord told me he was raising the rent. After everything that had happened, the little coastal town in New

Hampshire where I'd grown up had begun to take on a post-cardlike quality in my mind–the sun on the water, the sound of seagulls, the sand that crept from the beach onto the streets—it all seemed so comforting, inviting even.

However, by the time I'd arrived, the tourist season was over. Stores were boarded up, and all of the summer people were gone. I had forgotten how depressing the quiet, deserted beaches could be, how the whole place would close in on it-self. I'd forgotten the real reason I'd left. My mother had of-fered me the room, but I'd ducked the topic, told her that I already had a place to stay. Since then, I had been dodging her calls and doing everything I could to keep from coming close to my house. At times, it was almost interesting trying to stay off certain streets, but it was as though I was waiting for some-thing. Nights, I lay in bed listening to a house full of people sleep. Just being in town again was giving me insomnia. I'd lost weight. I was drifting further away from the person I had been not even a month earlier, and it scared me.

I decided to lie to Loames about my mother. "She needed the money," I said. "And she wouldn't take it from me."

I unlocked the front door with the spare key my mother had left in the mailbox and led Loames inside. The house was dark, but I could hear a radio playing upstairs. I stepped into the living room and switched on a lamp. Walking in there was like walking onto a stage, a combination of fear and tension as well as release. I was finally back.

All of the furniture was exactly the same, only it had been pushed into the center of the room. Some ragged strips of old wallpaper were lying on the floor. The rest was stuffed into a garbage bag. On the far end of the longest wall the words, "Edith Drogan's uncle is dead" were scrawled in a wide and listing hand, like it had been written by a child or a drunk. Because it was squeezed near the corner, the message looked oddly small and misplaced. The letters appeared to hover over the plaster.

"You do that?" Loames asked. He was wandering around the room, checking it out.

"No. I grew up here, but we never took down the wallpaper that the last family left. I didn't even know that was there."

"Well, someone wanted people to know that this guy was dead."

"I guess so."

My mother had hired a handyman to come and hang the wallpaper for her. She was just trying to save money by taking what was there down herself so she wouldn't have to pay him to do it. She said the glue was so old that the paper practically fell off the wall in her hands. But she hadn't noticed the writing when the wallpaper was coming down. Turning around and seeing it, though, was like turning around and finding a stranger in the room. "All I wanted was a little change, and look what happened," she said. "Now I find out that the people who lived here before us were the kind of people who wrote crazy things on the walls. I don't want to think that those kind of people have lived in my house. I feel like I've been missing something for all these years."

Her voice was angry, blunt, as though she was defending herself against the very words on the wall. It was a familiar tone, the same one that had convinced me so many years earlier that I should never tell my mother anything that she would not want to hear. At the moment when my life had unhinged itself from what I knew it to be, it was her voice that proved to me that, whatever was wrong, she did not want to know. Unlike my mother, seeing the message on the wall didn't shock me. It only reminded me of everything I'd tried to cover over, of the part of myself I had attempted to bury by moving away.

"Are we rolling this paper out on the floor or what?" Loames asked.

"Oh, um, there might be a folding table we could use out in the carport," I said. I felt a twinge, the sudden pulse of a memory. Upstairs, something dropped and rolled across the floor. We could hear a muffled swear.

Loames glanced at the ceiling, then back to me. "Okay, then. It's your house," he said. "Lead the way."

RAIN WAS battering the green corrugated roof of the carport and streaming in through the gaps between it and the walls. The smell of oil and wet boxes hadn't been drawn out by the wind. Loames moved past me and began poking around. He seemed almost too eager about helping, but I wasn't going to complain. Having him there would cut in half the time I'd have to spend in the house, and that was good enough for me.

"I don't see any table, but we could use those," Loames said, and nodded to a pair of old sawhorses stuck behind a pile of beach chairs. "And that," he said, pointing to a sheet of plywood that was resting atop the crossbeams overhead. "That'll work. I'll get the sawhorses," Loames said. "You get that plywood."

"Fine," I said, still standing in the doorway. That was all I could manage to say. It would be an easy task, but Loames had no idea what he was asking.

Eight years before my father's death, I had almost killed him there in the carport. For years, I had squeezed that memory out of my mind. Now it seemed like the only one I had. I held my breath, took a step inside. There was a ladder resting against the wall, and I had to use it to reach the rafters. Once I was up there, I looked down, gauging the distance. Seeing the sheer drop, a good ten or eleven feet, I was amazed that my father had survived.

It happened when I was seventeen. I'd gone to get a can of spray paint down from the rafters where I'd stored it because I had wanted to spray my name onto the back of a toolbox. When I went into the carport, my father was lying under his truck on a dolly replacing tie rods and singing to himself. He hadn't heard me come in. It had been months since he'd gone deaf in his left ear, and the right one was already following fast, but my father still sang. Only now he would sing softly, in a whisper I didn't believe him capable of, as if he didn't want to overhear himself.

That was not the man I knew. To say my father had a bad temper was like saying water is wet; that's only part of it. He was not a big man, but it was as if the sound of his voice could shake the walls and rattle the dishes in the cabinets like a train plowing through the house. His problem wasn't a short fuse; it was the lack of one altogether. I never knew what would set him off. It could have been anything: a cold meal, a leaky faucet, a look. Living in anticipation of what might happen next was like walking around with a vase balanced on my head, and it had left me with a permanent cramp. When the doctor told my father that his hearing was going, I had to wonder whether it wasn't the intensity of his own voice that had made him deaf.

That day in the carport, I knew my father hadn't noticed me. I was happy to have slipped past his radar and just wanted to get out of range as quickly as I could. I got up on the ladder and reached for the spray paint, steadying myself by holding one of the crossbeams. A few gallon-sized cans of paint and a coil of rope were balanced across the plank. When I touched it, the crossbeam shook, and one can of paint teetered near the edge, enough for me to see that it wasn't stable.

I nudged the crossbeam again just to watch the can shiver. Seeing it tremble over my father's head made my lungs feel full. I could finally feel myself breathing. All that summer I'd been hiding from him, moving from one room to the next right before he would come in. It seemed like every time he saw me there would be a fight. I would catch hell for not locking the front door or for leaving the television on, anything. Afterwards, my father would grab me by the face with one hand, eyeing me, ready to read my lips for any curse or back talk. "My roof. My rules," he would say, and point at the ceiling, then himself, as though I was the one who couldn't hear.

I gave the beam another push. I couldn't help myself. It was as if I was getting back at him, even though he had no sense of what I was doing. A bushing rolled across the floor from underneath the truck, and I froze. My father slid out to get it, oblivious to my presence, but knocked it further away. He was still singing, only more slowly as he held out his arm.

Some renegade emotion began to spread through my body,

burning up into my head and leaking down into my arms. Nothing about my father seemed real or mattered. I took one look at his face as it rested on the cement floor and jabbed the crossbeam with everything I had.

I remembered seeing the paint can fall, infinitely, painfully, slowly. It was like I could hear it arcing and cutting through the air. I remembered gazing down at my father, seeing his arm outstretched, still grasping for the bushing, then realizing that whatever it was that had been coursing through me had dissolved completely.

It wasn't until I went back into the house that I perceived the size of what I had done. The paint can had hit my father in the head, knocking him unconscious, and in a daze, I'd left him lying there in the carport. Inside, my mother was sitting at the kitchen table buttering a piece of toast, the knife rasping over the hardened bread. When my body finally began to register what had happened, I had to hold onto the counter to keep from shaking. The floor kept rearing up beneath my feet. The sound of the knife echoed in my ears. Then my mother spoke to me.

"Was the paper out there?" she asked. I stared at her. She must have thought that I had gone out for it, then come back in through the side door.

"If it wasn't, I wouldn't be surprised. Somebody's been stealing it," she announced, slicing into the butter. "I think it's that man who moved in across the street. But don't tell your father or he'll wring his neck. Poor man has to steal other people's papers. It's a shame, really."

My mother was acting so serious that I had to remind myself that she was talking about someone she was barely acquainted with. It was as if she was embarrassed, as though the neighbor's small problem, real or imagined, was too much for her to bear. Anything I could have said at that moment would have been unbelievable to her, completely beyond what she could accept. With those words, I realized that I couldn't tell her. Not ever.

My mother set her knife down and said, "I've been trying not to think about it."

"CAN WE use these?" Loames asked. He'd been rummaging through the carport and had found a bucket full of rollers and brushes, which he held up for me to see. The light coming through the green roofing looked so thick on his pale shirt and skin that it seemed like he should feel it. I lifted the sheet of plywood from the rafters and set it down against the ladder. "Sure," I said. "Whatever."

Loames lifted one sawhorse onto each shoulder and snapped up the bucket of brushes. He made it up the steps into the house carrying everything, then a leg on one of the sawhorses got caught on the door frame.

"Can you give me a hand?" he called.

As I watched Loames try to free himself, time slowed to a near stop, just as it had when my father reached for the bushing. Both of my parents would later call what had happened in the carport an accident. That was all they believed it could have been, and I never said otherwise.

Loames shifted and the leg slipped free. "Never mind," he said, and went inside.

The paint can had badly broken my father's jaw. It had to be wired shut, and he was unable to speak for nearly a month. During that time, I tried not to act guilty and pretended not to enjoy the solid silence that filled the house. My mother tended to my father, keeping him in bed most of the time and feeding him his meals through a straw. I figured that she was probably as grateful for the reprieve as I was. My mother and I had never been close, not even in the way a mother and son should have been, and when we talked, it was only what needed to be said. Like any reflex, our conversations lacked much thought. But in those weeks, I became aware of how similarly we moved in the then quiet house, how we were both soaking up the stillness, and how neither of us chose to mention the fact that my father would soon be well enough to talk. We were not alike,

I'd decided, though we were far from different. Maybe that was the way it was supposed to be.

I followed Loames inside. He was already setting up the makeshift table. The living room felt damp. The stains on the walls from the old wallpaper glue looked like watermarks. It was as if the room had been flooded at one time, and the message was floating above the waterline. I unrolled a section of the wallpaper my mother had chosen, and the ends curled up, revealing a turquoise background patterned with feathers and flowers and vines. It looked like a view of some enchanted lagoon in a dream, but from the bottom up.

Measuring out the sheets and applying the glue was easy enough, and Loames and I could do it quickly. Lining up the paper, however, and getting it on the wall properly took time and concentration. I brought in a chair from the kitchen to stand on, and I held the tops of the sheets while Loames secured the bottoms, then both of us worked to lay on the wallpaper without any wrinkles. The sound of Loames's steady breathing relaxed me, so much so that when the shriek of bursting glass came from upstairs, I jumped. Heavy footsteps followed. Furniture was being dragged across the floor.

"This a friend of your mother's?" Loames asked, tracing the sound of the steps across the ceiling with his eyes.

"No. She didn't know him. I've never met him either."

I tried to guess what my mother would have done if she had been there to hear the ruckus. Probably very little. When my father's temper would flare, she would sit down and stare straight ahead while he yelled, her face a blank mask. At those times, I noticed a kind of dullness and distance in her eyes, like she had willed herself into a trance. She seemed not to hear what was being said and, in that way, could listen for as long as it took.

"I guess your mother really needed the money," Loames said.

THE AFTERNOON was darkening, and the rain had become light, but constant. By then, we'd wallpapered more than half of the room. Scraps sat in mounds on the floor. The glue was running low, but Loames said he thought we would have enough to finish.

"I've done whole rooms with less than this," he told me.

It was clear that he wanted me to respond, but I wasn't sure how.

"Yeah, I've wallpapered a bunch of rooms," Loames continued, rolling out a thin layer of paste on the paper and glancing up at me hopefully.

"Oh really?" I tried. "Where?"

"I used to own a little motel up by the highway. It was a sweet deal when I bought it. Thought I could do good business during the summers."

Loames turned his eyes to the wall. He was resisting whatever expression he truly wanted to make. I kept working, pressing down the paper and pretending not to notice, then suddenly the radio upstairs was blaring. Loames's face broke. He shouted at the ceiling, "Be quiet, damn it. You shut up, up there."

I felt the air get thick the way it did when a thunderstorm was coming in off the bay, the same way it would feel when my father would enter a room. I waited, but there was no response from above. Loames shook his head.

"Anyway," he said, recomposing himself, "my motel had a pool. And it had underwater lights. The lights didn't work, but I planned on fixing them. And there were shag carpets in every room and mini-fridges. It was pretty nice for a little cinder block building. Had a few old ladies who kept the volume up on their televisions and some illegals left over from working the summer rush, but they were all good people. You know, paid their bills on time."

Another sheet of wallpaper was ready to go and Loames picked it up, so I followed his lead, letting him talk.

"But there was this one guy," he said, his voice growing

strained. "The housekeeper told me his sheets and towels were always burned and black and full of holes. When she went in to vacuum his room, there were scorch marks on the rug. One of the illegals told me he'd seen the guy spray hairspray on his jeans and light them with a match. He said the guy liked to watch himself burn. Whenever I'd see him, the guy's clothes were singed and falling apart."

I didn't know where this story was going, and Loames wasn't giving me the opportunity to change the subject or interrupt. I was afraid to try. Finishing the room as quickly as possible was all I could hope to do.

We'd been working around the room, unconsciously leaving the message for last. One of the next two sheets would cover it. I held a piece of the paper between my fingers, testing its thickness, as though it might not be capable of concealing the writing. I imagined that the words would still be visible through the paper, the long scrawl rising between the petals and leaves. Whatever the message really meant was lost on me. I could easily guess–somebody was dead–but that was so simple it seemed wrong. There was a story behind those words, only it was as unfamiliar as the handwriting. Even so, the message felt important, like it needed to be there on the wall.

My mother was right to feel as though she'd been missing something, though it had nothing to do with what was written in our living room. After so many years, hidden but always there, the message spoke to my mother and to me. It did what I never could.

Loames was running his hands over the paper slowly, almost tenderly. His face was close to the wall. So when the door slammed upstairs, he nearly smashed his nose. My muscles went stiff, an old habit of preparation. A second later, Loames grabbed the chair out from under me and put his lips up to the ceiling vent. "I can hear you," he shouted. "I told you to shut up, but I can still hear you."

I waited again, expecting the tenant to either shout back or come pounding down the stairs. Loames appeared to be waiting for that too. But there was nothing, no reaction. After a minute, Loames came down off the chair and moved it back into position to finish the section of wallpaper. Sighing, he took up his story right where he had left off.

"Eventually, people's clothes were being stolen off their laundry lines. It was obvious who the culprit was. So at that point, I said to myself, 'Self, it's time to step in.' I talk to the guy, and he's agreeable about the whole thing. Says it won't happen again. But get this. That same night, he pours a can of oil into the pool and lights it. Crazy, right? Nuts. When I go to his room, all of his stuff's gone. I'll tell you, that fire burned for hours, and I couldn't do a damn thing but wait until it died out."

I began to back away from Loames. Standing next to him felt risky, like standing next to a wild animal. But he was oblivious. He was doing all of the work by himself, lining up the edges and forcing out air pockets. With his eyes fixed on the wallpaper, he reminded me of someone staring at the ocean, trying to see past the light on the surface.

"The next day, after the fire burned out, I went to buy some tile to redo the pool. I found this kind with mermaids on them and fish spouting water. The tiles were good-looking. Cute, you know," Loames said, then he paused. "When I came back, the fire trucks were already leaving. The place looked like one of those photo negatives. The cinder block was all black from the smoke, and the doors and the roof were white because you could see the cloudy sky through them. Everything was gone."

I watched as tears made their way down Loames's pitted cheeks. I was at a complete loss. Even though the man made me uncomfortable, at that moment I would have told him whatever he wanted to hear. But I couldn't even conceive of what that might be.

"I had that tile for years," Loames said, wiping his eyes. "I couldn't sell it. And the distributor wouldn't buy it back. I guess I'm the only one who ever wanted tiles with mermaids on them."

The last section of paper was ready to go up, but Loames had gone over to the window to collect himself. His arms were hanging at his sides like he had lost all feeling in them. I raised the piece myself. The previous one had only covered a few letters of the message. This one would blot out the rest.

Before I could get both corners tacked down, there was a crash upstairs. I felt a shudder in the wall, and the paper fell to the floor. It sounded like the tenant had thrown his television across the room.

Loames didn't move for a few seconds. When he did, it was at the solemn pace of a man who intended to do real harm. Of all the looks I had seen play across my father's face, this one was utterly foreign. Without a word, Loames disappeared up the stairs. And I let him go.

Even though my eyes were open, I felt like I couldn't see because I was listening so hard. It had gone silent upstairs. I sat down on the chair and stared at the spot where Loames had stood. I heard noises, but the sound was more muffled than before. My head was throbbing. I was sweating and shivering all at once. If there was one person who knew this feeling as well as I did, it was my mother. I'd always wondered how things had been when she was alone with my father, if he was ever different. Once, I'd watched them together through a window as they worked in the garden. My father saw that my mother's hands were dirty, and he took off his work gloves, shook them clean, and gave them to her to wear. I held that image of them in my mind as I sat there waiting for Loames in the living room I hadn't been inside of in fourteen years. Then I thought of my empty room at the boardinghouse, and I was struck by how little my life had changed.

THERE WERE no other cars on the road as Loames drove us back. The streetlights had come on, but only every other one worked. Loames was holding the steering wheel firmly, taking the turns slow and wide. It was like I was riding in the front seat of a taxicab with the driver. I could tell that Loames didn't want to be around me, at least not anymore.

"Maybe you should tell your mother to find somebody else to rent to," he said. "It's not good to have people like that in your house. You never know with them."

"I'll tell her that."

Loames stopped in front of the boardinghouse and left the car running. I hesitated, then said, "Well, thanks. For the help, I mean."

I opened the car door carefully, got out, and leaned in again, trying to think of something else I could add. The rain blew against my back and spattered the car seat. After a minute, Loames said, "That seat's getting wet."

"Oh," I said. "Sorry."

Loames let his foot off the brake, causing the car to move. I had no choice but to shut the door. I watched Loames make a U-turn, then drive off, and I tried to see his face through the foggy windows. I wondered, was I glimpsing a vision of my life years in the future, one of a number of possibilities. If this was it, I wasn't sure whether to be scared or thankful for the chance to see it.

When the rain forced me inside, I went and sat on the rusted glider in the screened-in porch. The porch smelled like an old rowboat, rotten and waterlogged, and the screens were warped, which made everything outside appear to be vibrating.

After a few minutes, a tall, stern-faced black man stepped onto the porch holding a mug of coffee. He stood by the door. "That Loames's car I heard?" he asked.

I nodded and rocked the glider.

"What'd he help you do?"

"What?"

"I had a pair of pants. They were too long," the man said, rubbing one side of the mug to warm his hand. "Loames offered to sew the bottoms up for me. He came to my room with a needle and thread. Did a real neat job. Then he told me about his burned-down motel. Another guy warned me about Loames. But I wanted the pants fixed, so I listened to his story. Somebody else got him to repair a typewriter for them."

I kept rocking, squeezing the faded cushion beneath me until I lost the sensation of the fabric.

"Don't worry," the man told me. "It's a one-time deal with Loames. He won't bug you again. He won't even talk to you now that he's told you. You're off the hook."

It was cold out on the porch, and I could see the man's breath even after he spoke. Night was coming on. The rain was turning to sleet. I remembered thinking that I was looking forward to the first snowfall at home, to seeing the snow on the beach. That might have been the one thing I truly wanted to come back for. It had always amazed me to watch the tiny flakes of snow piling up over the grains of sand and to see the shape of the dunes rising beneath the cover of the drifts. The past was like that, one thing overlapping another, with the bottom layer always pressing itself through.

I tried to concentrate on the motion of the glider, letting my head sway as it moved. My mother would call as soon as she got back from the church. I told myself that I should go inside and wait. It would be better to stay near the phone, to be right there, close by.

One Train May Hide Another

WHEN YOU OPEN your eyes, you are unable to remember the name of the city you are in. You see a man walking a camel around the cars that are stopped in the dusty, crowded street. That should help to jog your memory, but it doesn't. You consider asking your father where you are, then you think better of it. He has already told you once, and you don't want to bother him. He looks busy.

He has brought you with him on a business trip, and together you stand in the shade of an awning, hiding from the blistering sun while he flips through his date book. You can see notes scribbled in under the dates and you try to read them. You would like to know what your father writes in this book of his, but you can't make out any of the words. They don't even look like English. Your father, you decide, has bad handwriting.

"This is flypaper weather," your father says. "The heat just sticks to you. Aren't you glad we don't live here?" He is trying to be funny.

"Very," you say, because you believe you are supposed to answer.

You look for the man with the camel, but he is gone, lost

in the traffic. The fumes of idling trucks and motor scooters stream in the hot wind. Nearby on the corner, a small fire is burning in an open metal drum. Flies and sand and bits of burned paper spin through the air, and when you feel something stick to you, you slap your skin as though you have been bitten.

"Here," your father says, pushing the suitcases beside your leg. He cups his hand over his eyes. "Watch these for a second while I look for a taxi. I'm dying for a shower."

You imagine that the hotel where you are staying will be depressing. The foreign ones usually are. It will be the best hotel in the city, because your father will only stay where he is assured everything is the best, but the beds will probably be hard and there may be no television or carpet.

Your father has taken you out of school in order for you to accompany him on his trip. Since your mother's death more than a year ago, he has done this regularly. So much so that you have given up complaining. In the past five months, you have been to Singapore, Berlin, and Las Vegas. You like collecting the small wrapped soaps and matchbooks from the various hotels, but you have never really wanted to take any of the trips. Now, surrounded by all of your luggage, you feel you could hate your father for constantly making you go, for being selfish about you and loving you in the way that he does. But you don't hate him. You feel bad for him. He is always looking at you as though you are about to disappear. And sometimes you worry that it could actually happen.

"No luck," your father says. "I guess we should walk around for awhile, and then we'll find one."

"Where are we again?" you ask.

"I told you, sweetie. We're in Marrakech. It's a famous place, sort of. Lots of history." He picks up your suitcases. "Give me your hand," he says, and makes room for your arm inside his.

As you walk through the warren of narrow, whitewashed lanes, your fingers slide down your father's arm until you are holding him by the wrist. Once, you remember, his hands smelled of wood smoke when they brushed past your cheek. You are not sure why that was, and it makes you wonder about him. You have no real conception of what your father does when he is alone, and you believe you may never find out.

Women shrouded in robes are selling fruit out of baskets. Skinny dogs roam the alleys. When a breeze finally blows, the sound of tiny bells tinkling on wind chimes outlasts the feeling of coolness brought with the wind.

"How about we stop for a drink?" your father asks, a drop of sweat creeping down his face. "We could use it. We can grab a taxi later, right?"

"Okay," you answer, trying to keep up.

"Over there," he says, gesturing toward the red neon sign shaped like a wineglass that is hanging in a window. "I bet that place'll have drinks. That or they sell glasses."

When you enter the arched doorway, you realize that you are in a bar. You have never been in a bar before, but you have seen them on television. This one looks nothing like the ones on TV. It appears to have been hollowed out of a mountain. The ceiling curves down into pillars, and the chairs are built into the walls. The thick scent of incense mingles with cigarette smoke, which hangs above the room like a layer of clouds. Your arm is still pinned beneath your father's, and he is pulling you along behind him.

"I guess we're going to have to rely on my high school French lessons," he says, piling your suitcases against the bar, then he pats your shoulder reassuringly.

"Pardon, monsieur," your father says to get the bartender's attention. The bartender, whose bony face renders him with a permanent scowl, sets down the newspaper he is reading. Cheerfully, your father continues, "Me fille et moi, nous avons très soif. Qu'est-que vous avez boire?"

The bartender answers quickly, throwing your father off. He stutters and stumbles over his words and finally resorts to pointing. You understand that he has ordered Cokes for both of you.

"Il est très facile!" your father says to you. "That was easy."

He pulls a stool over for you, then takes one for himself. The bartender passes you your drinks and returns to his paper. He does not want to be bothered with you or your father. You notice that there is only one other man at the bar, a few seats down. He has a wide, leather-bound book open in front of him. After a few minutes, you realize that he is not turning the pages. Because his head is down, you can't tell if he is reading at all. You decide that he is praying. To you, praying seems a lot like gambling. You have walked through a casino in Las Vegas with your father, and there you saw that the people all had the same look of concentration on their faces as people in prayer. Once you tried praying for a pair of roller skates for Christmas, but you didn't get them. You don't understand why anyone would bother praying if it doesn't work every time.

"I never thought a Coke could taste this good," your father announces.

There are times when you do not know what to say to your father. He is always making small talk. He tells you that it is part of his job: "Small talk for small minds." But everything he says seems to require a response, and you are never sure whether you are giving the right one.

"Me neither," you reply, but your answer is lost under the whining sort of music that is playing on a transistor radio. Then you hear a voice ask, "No one could have suggested a better bar to you than this one?"

A man appears behind you as if from out of nowhere. Your father stiffens, puts his foot against your suitcases.

"I am sorry," the man says. "Maybe I am too forward?" He is clean-shaven and well dressed in a shirt and slacks, but you are aware that you can smell his breath. "You do not know me," he continues, "and I do not mean to scare you. But I heard you speaking English, and I like to practice when I can get the chance. My name is Ahmet."

He shakes hands with your father vigorously, then nods at you.

"You are not on holiday?" Ahmet asks, appraising your father's suit. "It is business then?"

Your father edges closer to you while Ahmet explains that he went to school and learned English in Cairo with British professors, so he speaks with a slight British accent, which he is proud of. He lives here now, he tells you, with his father, working in his silver shop.

"Yes, beautiful silver trinkets and goblets. Many lovely things. You should come and see them. I can show you."

A salesman, you think. You hope that Ahmet won't ask your father if he wants to buy a gift for his wife. Because that might bring your father to tears. It has happened before.

"No, no, okay," Ahmet says, "I do not mean to be like that. Pushy? That is the word? No. I am only offering. Never mind. You can never mind."

Standing, your father says, "Look, my daughter and I are very tired. I don't mean to be rude, but it's been a long day."

You feel there is something missing from his voice.

"Yes, yes." Ahmet backs away, but just a little. "I am only asking because I thought maybe you were here, in this bar, for the other reason. You are not, are you, here for *that*?"

From the expression on your father's face, you think Ahmet must be talking about something dirty. Before you were born, your father came home early one day and found a strange man hiding in your mother's closet. Luckily, he was able to lock the man in there until the police came. Later, they told him that the man had probably been waiting for a woman to come home so he could take her by surprise. You have heard the story so many times that you have memorized the last line as if it were the punch line to a joke. "We had a lunatic in our house," your father will say. "A lunatic in our very own closet."

Ahmet leans in and whispers, "The gold. That is what I'm talking of."

Confused, your father frowns. His lips pull tightly over his teeth, and his jaw is working as if he is chewing some invisible food. He seems different to you, like someone you don't recognize. You try to picture what you must look like next to one another, you and this man you resemble, but only vaguely.

"You know, maybe you have a thing that you like very much, but you would like it better if it was gold." Ahmet raises his eyebrows. "In English, the word is. . . ." He snaps his fingers repeatedly, then blurts, "Alchemy!" He checks to see if anybody else is listening. "Alchemy," he whispers.

Your father puts out one of his hands as if to stop him. The other finds your back. "I don't know what you're getting at mister, but–"

Ahmet starts in again softly. "Surely you know what I mean, or why else would you be here, in this bar. But if you want to act like you do not know, then that is fine." He glances around, nodding. "I see. That is what you prefer. I will tell you then, and you will have to say nothing. My father, he will do it. He will do most anything smaller than a melon. And snakes and pigeons. But his specialty is canaries. Beautiful golden canaries and golden cages. The cage would be only a little money, but the canaries cost much. They are delicate to begin with."

You are holding your breath because you think it will make you hear this man more clearly. You lean forward slightly and feel your father's hand slip off your shoulder. His face goes slack.

"If you have brought something with you, he must see it beforehand. Not everything can be done." Ahmet turns and looks at you. Then you realize that he is talking about you. His face convinces you that he is serious, and the awful fear that you are unreal or could be made so rolls through you like a rock slide.

Ahmet lowers his voice confidentially. "As I said, not everything can be done."

Your father grabs your suitcases and pushes you off the stool. "Stay away from us," he shouts, forcing you toward the door.

You turn back in time to see Ahmet watching you and your father leave, stunned by your sudden departure, unsure what he has done.

Outside, a single taxi sits at the end of the alley. Your father runs to get it, dragging you behind him. He shows the driver a paper with your hotel's address on it, then throws the cases in the backseat, forcing you in along with them. He glances over his shoulder and crowds in beside you.

As the taxi lumbers through the streets, your father begins to relax. He rubs his face and loosens the damp part of his shirt from his back.

"Did he mean that about the canaries?" you ask.

"No," your father says. "He was crazy. Forget about it. He was a crazy man."

"What did he mean, then?"

Your father shifts toward the window, ignoring the question.

You know what will happen once you are at the hotel. Your father will shower quickly, and you will sit and wait while the two of you take turns using the bathroom. When both of you are finished, your father will talk about other things, like what you should order from room service or which bed you have chosen, as though the bar and what happened there will cease to exist in your memory because he refuses to talk about it. You cannot help but think that, in this way, your father has tried to erase whole pieces of the world for you. You do not know if this is a bad thing or not.

Soon you drive past a train that is stopped on the tracks. Men are unloading the train cars, doubled over under the weight of the sacks they are carrying. Above the train, a sign strung on a rope reads, in three languages, English at the bottom, "One Train May Hide Another."

The driver inches forward, closer to the tracks. You try, but you cannot see the end of the train or beyond it to where another one would come from. Your own life will be like this, you think, not nearly predictable, and now you realize that you are in possession of that secret, one that you will be responsible for forever.

The taxi moves past the train and falls in with the rest of the traffic as the car enters an open, sun-washed square. In the center of the square, a mob of children encircles a group of tourists. The children grope the tourists and hold their palms up for change.

Your father shakes his head. "Can you believe that?" he asks. "These kids, who aren't even half your age, are begging for money. Their parents make them do it. Because they're young and cute and pitiful looking."

He cranks up his window. "Once, a bunch of kids like those came up to me. They were holding out newspapers. I thought they were trying to sell them, but really they were using them to cover up their hands so they could go for my wallet. One of them tried to grab my briefcase. He didn't even have any shoes."

Your father leans back, allowing you to see past him. "Don't you feel lucky that you don't have to live like that?"

You wish you hadn't seen this. The sun is right in your eyes, and it is as if you have been carefully watching a slide show in a dark room and the screen has suddenly gone white. There are things that you do not want to know, infinite merciless facts that you will have to know. Everything is waiting for you, taking on its own weight.

"Yes," you tell him. "I'm lucky."

Soon you will leave this city and you will be back in America. There you will change, and all of your memories will stay the same, not responsible for being any different.

"We'll be going home in a couple of days," your father says. "We'll be there before you know it."

You nod as the tourists and the children are swept deeper into the closing crowd. Then you and your father stare out opposite windows until the taxi begins to move.

Unemployment

AS A FAVOR to my father, I was living with my brother. I'd been evicted from my apartment and sleeping in my car, but according to my father, I was the one who was helping Desmond out by moving in with him.

My brother was on the verge of something–good or bad, I didn't know–and whatever it was, it kept him up nights. I'd been there twelve days, and each morning I'd wake up and find him, exhausted but almost giddy, already at work on a new project. Tuesday it was the refrigerator. We were supposed to be cleaning it, but Desmond had to empty the shelves first. "Time's up. Hit the road," he said, addressing each individual container as though it had personally offended him. Even the food that hadn't expired yet got the drill sergeant treatment.

"Let me ask you a question, Frank," he said, standing next to the refrigerator, a wet rag in hand. "Are you going to help or are you going to sit there and stare?"

"Do I have a choice?" I asked. He didn't answer.

Desmond didn't like to be watched. Not since he got out of prison. So I got up to help him. There wasn't room for both of us in front of the refrigerator. Instead, I went to the sink and started to empty the cartons that were sitting on the drainboard into the garbage.

"That's the ticket." Desmond slapped my back. "Dump all the really rancid stuff and save whatever's semi-edible. I'll feed it to the dogs."

The dogs were another of Desmond's projects. He had created what he called a "refuge" in the backyard. He kept over twenty dogs in a pen that he'd built spanning the length of the property. Most were strays, but I had a feeling that he'd gotten too excited about the idea and started luring dogs out of people's yards. One day I came across a drawer full of tags. When I asked him about it, my brother's response was, "*Stray dog* is a subjective term."

Like Desmond's other projects, I figured the dog thing was probably only temporary. My first day at his place, he'd started repainting the inside of the house. He'd paint dead bugs into the corners of windows, saying, "Sucks to be you," then he'd skip whole walls. Desmond was working on cleaning out the gutters too–that was until one corner on the front of the house snapped loose. He tried reattaching the gutter with some rope, but gave up midway through and left the thing hanging like a broken arm in a sling. My brother had enough money squirreled away to buy a place of his own, but his current house was a rental. I was just waiting for my second notice of eviction.

My counselor at the unemployment office said that all my moving around was one of the things preventing me from getting a steady job. She was right, of course, but I had no intention of telling her that. It was the moving, my sloppy resume, my rumpled suits, my attitude. I'd given up, and there was no hiding it. After seven months of cashing government checks, I fully understood what it meant to be out of work. It had made me cynical. I knew what I was missing, and I knew my options. Both depressed me.

I'd quit or been fired from every job that came my way–fast food, stocking boxes, even a night shift at a poultry plant. I told the manager that sorting chicken parts was mind-numbing, soul-crushing work, and he said, "Maybe, but you can't sue us for that." Then he told me to clean out my locker. After that, my father set me up with a part-time spot at a locksmith's shop, and I broke a press on purpose, obligating the man to let me go. It wasn't that I didn't want to work. I just didn't want to work for anyone in particular. I'd envisioned myself with a career and had always assumed that one day the right job would find me. However, nothing had turned up. I thought I was too good for menial labor, and, at the time, I didn't mind saying so. I was an idea man, and nobody appreciated that.

When my father found out about the press, he called in his favor and told me to go and stay with Desmond. He'd visited him and seen the "refuge" and the disassembled appliances and the rows of random pens that were arranged, by color, on the living room floor. It made him nervous. He said he didn't want his son going off the deep end in an empty house. His last words to me were, "Desmond's got to snap out of it." I moved in the very next day.

"Should I save this for the dogs?" I asked, holding up an open tub of onion dip that had a fuzzy, faint green frosting.

"Dogs are smart. They'll eat around that."

"Yeah, and if dogs had a middle finger they'd be giving it to you right now."

Desmond was tuning me out. He opened the crisper, then the smell of spoiled food shot up like a spike. A wedge of cheese, downy with white mold, sat alone in the drawer.

"Are we going to save that for the dogs?" I asked.

"Right. Then I'd have even more of those animal activists harassing me."

In general, the neighbors thought Desmond was crazy but harmless, the male equivalent of a nutty old lady with a hundred cats. They occasionally complained about the barking, but nobody really seemed to mind the refuge except for one older Asian woman who didn't even live nearby. We knew her by her car, a battered hatchback that had Woodstock bumper stickers all over it. She came once a week to put out flyers and notes threatening to call the police about Desmond's make-shift pound.

"Did you see the last thing that lady left on the fence?" He handed me a pamphlet from the table. It was about animal cruelty, and it was full of photos of monkeys being tortured and of a man squeezing drops into a rabbit's eye. "I don't do that," Desmond shouted, shaking the wet rag. "I don't put junk in the dogs' eyes. Hell, I give them bones and Frisbees and shit."

Desmond had never met the woman, only seen her from the window as she was driving away, but he talked about her constantly. "She's a real hardnose," he would say. "Stone cold. I can tell. So cold that she can only relate to animals, less evolved species." Once he got onto the subject of this lady, it was hard to get him off it. He was like someone who was trying not to act drunk. He spoke normally and walked straight, but it took effort.

"You know what I would say to that lady if I met her?" Desmond asked, slamming the refrigerator door. "I'd say, 'Lady, I know what it's like to be locked up, and these dogs have it good. They have it better than most. So you can kiss this," he declared, pointing to his ass.

Desmond had gone to prison a year earlier for smoothing out the books on a string of chop shops, and because he was too scared to hand over any of the bigger names involved, he did the full sentence. Desmond had let two men who stole cars for a living convince him that polishing their balance sheets wasn't really illegal, but he didn't have a record, so he got off pretty easy. He was sent upstate to a minimum security facility, mostly white-collar embezzlers and tax evaders playing Ping-Pong and reading the *Times*. Shortly after going in, he started corresponding with a woman named Suzanne who said she was doing research for a psychology degree and wanted some real feedback on the emotional affect of prison life. She encouraged Desmond to call her collect and eventually mailed him a picture of herself. Then photocopies of poems, clippings of his horoscope, and romantic predictions from fortune cookies. As far as I knew, my brother had never really been in love before, not enough to consider marriage, but within a few months he proposed, and Suzanne accepted. When Desmond told her to start planning their honeymoon, explaining that he'd be released by spring, she backed down. Apparently, Suzanne thought Desmond was going to be in prison for a lot longer than a year, and when she found out otherwise, she changed her mind and quit communicating with him altogether. How's that for emotional affect?

With the refrigerator now empty, Desmond began scrubbing the shelves. This was my cue to take a break. Then the phone rang. Desmond's face dropped. We'd been getting a lot of hang-ups lately, and each time a call came in, he refused to answer it. He was convinced that it was Suzanne. He made me pick up, hoping that would force her to ask if he was there, if she had the correct phone number. Even though I doubted it was her, I kept telling him that my answering would only make her think she *did* have the wrong number, and then she wouldn't call back. "She knows it's the right one," he would declare. "She knows."

Truthfully, the hang-ups bothered me. Desmond wanted to believe that Suzanne would call. I was sure she wouldn't. I began to worry that it was someone I owed money to who was looking to collect or that it was one of the grand-auto-theft guys, out on parole and checking up on Desmond. He told me he didn't care if it was. "Let them break their fingers dialing," he'd say. I didn't argue. I figured that those sort of people didn't simply make prank calls.

The phone had rung twice, and Desmond was yelling at me to get it. As usual, when I picked up, the line was dead and buzzing in my ear. Desmond grabbed the freezer door and shook it furiously, but the whole thing looked comical instead of frightening.

"What are you going to do the next time the phone rings, Frank?" he demanded. "Ask . . . who . . . it . . . is." He enunciated each word, as though I didn't speak the language, then returned to wiping down the shelves in a huff.

Seeing my brother like this was too much for me. It wasn't him. In the time I'd been at his house, he'd hardly eaten. He slept in his clothes. His hair hung in his face, and his skin was always red and raw looking, like the blood was too close to the surface. Desmond looked like a zombie, and I couldn't stand it. I pictured him changing back to normal right before my eyes, like the woman in the box in a magic act who is cut in two, then restored, whole again. And there were times when it appeared as though the old Desmond had returned, sitting down, reading the want ads and circling possibilities, like his regular life was running late and he was killing time. Then he'd start repositioning all of the furniture to face south, and what seemed, momentarily, like magic would turn out to be a simple trick, an obvious sleight of hand.

After Desmond's outburst about the phone, I found I was still holding that pamphlet on animal cruelty. I noticed that it had the mailing address on it, a local one. I shoved the pamphlet into my pocket and told Desmond to put on his shoes. "We're going to run an errand," I said. "Come on."

"What?" He had his head in the refrigerator and was pretending like he couldn't hear me. "Did you *say* something, Frank?"

"I'm getting in the car. You're getting in the car. *We* are getting in the car."

Desmond sighed and padded out of the kitchen in search of his shoes, his posture a calm, unhurried slouch. In spite of his erratic behavior, my brother had basically become a pushover. Maybe that's what jail does to a person. Or maybe that's what being dumped does to a person. Who knew?

When we were on the road, Desmond was quiet, didn't even ask where we were going. I switched on the air-conditioner for no reason, then switched it off again. The sun was shining, and there was a breeze; it was the kind of weather that makes you want to put your hand out the window and roll your palm against the wind. I cranked down my window, but more to get rid of the smell of dirty clothes that permeated the car. It still looked like I was living in it. There was a heap of blankets on the backseat, a disposable razor on the dash, plastic silverware scattered on the floor. The ashtray was full too, which didn't help with the odor, and when I stopped at a light, I dumped the ashes out the window, reminding myself that I needed cigarettes. I'd quit, but living with Desmond had driven me back. There was a mini-mart up the street, so I pulled in.

"I gotta get a pack of smokes. You want anything? Something to drink?" I offered.

Desmond looked away, moping, trying to ignore me.

"Fine," I said. "Be right back. Don't take a walk on the yellow line while I'm gone."

Desmond rolled his eyes.

The mini-mart was long and dark and narrow like a box-car, and it was stocked from floor to ceiling. The teenage boy behind the counter was busy reading a comic book. The radio next to him was playing full blast. I grabbed Desmond a soda and went to the register for the cigarettes. The kid put his comic book down grudgingly. "What's it like outside, man?" he asked. "Is it hot?"

"No. It's okay. It's warm," I said. "It's perfect, actually."

"Yeah?" the kid said, as though that was bad news. "I gotta quit this job, man. Get me a job with some more windows."

The radio turned to static for a minute, and the kid looked at it. He took the comic book and smacked the radio with it until the music came in clearly. Then he raised the volume even higher. I thought about Desmond. I wanted to help him, but he'd lived with his heartache for so long, clocking in and out, morning and night, that I was afraid he'd miss it. He might be useless without it. The kid gave me my total for the soda, and by then, I'd forgotten about the cigarettes.

When I got back to the car, Desmond was fiddling with the side mirror, tilting it so it reflected the sky.

"No smokes?" he asked.

"Changed my mind," I said, handing him the can of soda.

"Now are you going to tell me where we're going?"

I showed Desmond the pamphlet with the woman's address on it. "I'm doing this for you," I said as I drove away from the mini-mart.

"Doing what? What are we doing?"

"You'll see."

"I don't want to see. I want to go home. I don't know what your problem is."

"My problem?"

"I feel fine. I feel perfectly ordinary."

I gave him a look. Desmond started to roll the soda between his palms, then tapped the lid but didn't open the can. We came out from under an overpass, and the sun caught on the hood, blinding both of us for an instant. Desmond closed his eyes and left them closed for a while.

"What are we going to do when we get there?" he finally asked. I didn't answer.

Desmond folded his arms. "I don't know anything about this lady except that she's Chinese and she's a fanatic. She's a Chinese fanatic. I wouldn't know what to say to someone like that. All I know about Chinese people is the stuff I saw in Charlie Chan movies."

"Charlie Chan was played by a white guy," I told him.

"My point exactly."

"Look, forget it. It's too late. We're already here."

I coasted down the street until I found the address, then parked on the opposite side of the road. The house was a low ranch-style job painted bright blue, and the car with all of the bumper stickers was sitting out front. The mailbox, which stood at the end of the driveway, had a picture of a basset hound on it.

"What did I tell you?" Desmond said. "A fanatic."

I turned off the engine and gave myself a minute to think. The truth was, I hadn't decided what we were going to do yet.

"Coming here is a bad idea," Desmond said. "It's retarded."

"Are you saying I'm retarded? I'm not retarded, Desmond. I'm an underachiever. There's a difference."

The window shades were drawn all over the house. It didn't

seem like anyone was home. Garbage bags ready for collection lined the street, and the only sound was the wind moving in the trees and rippling the bags.

"So what now, genius?" he asked. "Steal her flowers?"

Even with the car in the driveway, the house appeared to be empty, uninhabited. The thick screens made the windows look boarded up. There was no wreath on the door to take and no welcome mat to shred. The car with the bumper stickers was dented and in need of new paint job; we probably couldn't have done any noticeable damage to it without a wrecking ball. I considered telling Desmond to smash the windshield, but it would have made too much noise. Then I remembered that I had a kitchen knife in the glove compartment, a small piece of protection in case anybody I owed money to came sniffing around. When I got out the knife, Desmond's eyes locked on the blade, then traced a path from its tip, over my body, to my face.

"Let's go," I said, opening my door. Desmond wouldn't budge. "Get out of the car, I said."

I went around to his window, which was rolled all the way down, but he just sat there, shaking his head. His hands were on the window frame, one covering the lock. I set the knife on the hood and put my hands on my hips. "Do I have to pull you out, Desmond? Is that what I have to do? 'Cause I'll do it. Don't make me do it."

I had no intention of pulling him, couldn't even picture doing it in my mind, but saying that I would seemed to work. Desmond opened the door.

Glancing at the knife was enough to make him pick it up. He stared at it and held it loosely, like the knife might spring to life and he had to be ready to drop it at any time.

"What am I supposed to do?" Desmond asked.

"Do the tires," I said.

Desmond took a step back, but I held him. "What if it's the wrong house?" he asked.

"What do you mean the wrong house? This is it. This is

the address. That's the car. I'm right about this. Don't tell me I'm wrong, Desmond. This is the place. I'm insulted by your lack of confidence in me."

Desmond tried to pull away again. "Why? Why am I doing this?"

"Come on," I said. "All you ever talk about is this lady and how she's a cold, calculating lover of lower species. Don't you want to do something? Don't you want to show her who's boss? You've been cooped up in that house with those damn dogs for God knows how long. You're turning into a freak. You're turning into Rain Man. A little Judge Wapner and some Kmart and they can lock you up and throw away the key. Don't you just want to *do* something?" I squeezed his arm until he wrestled me off.

"I understand, Frank," Desmond said. "I get it now." He was squinting, as though he couldn't bear to see me all at once.

"I just want you to snap out of it," I said.

Desmond strode over to the car solemnly and plunged the knife into one of the back tires, then twisted it and yanked it out. He did the rest quickly, each with the same swift motion. It was my idea, but seeing him do it was like watching a stranger hit their child. I wasn't sure what to do with myself.

After he pulled the knife from the last tire, Desmond braced his hand on the roof of the car and slumped against the door as though he'd just run a couple of miles.

"Now how do you feel?" I asked. Desmond walked over to me, and we stood face to face. "You feel better, right?"

Then Desmond punched me square in the jaw. I fell back against my car with a thud. My ears were ringing, all I saw were stars, and it felt like my teeth were on fire. It took me a second to get my breath and figure out what had happened.

"Yeah, I do feel better," Desmond finally said. "Good idea, Frank."

I heard him get into my car and start the engine. When I could finally see straight, I crawled into the passenger seat, too ashamed of myself to speak. Desmond's soda was still sitting on the dashboard. He opened it and took a drink, putting the knife down in its place.

"Thanks for the soda," he said.

I rubbed my jaw. "No problem."

Desmond drove a few blocks, then we got caught behind a line of cars. Up ahead there had been an accident, and part of the road was blocked off, choking the traffic through a single lane. The police and ambulances were already on the scene. Two cars going in opposite directions had collided at an intersection. There was broken glass on the asphalt. One hubcap lay in the street. Both cars were damaged but not beyond repair.

Desmond took his hands off the wheel and leaned back. We were going to be there awhile. It was strange to see him driving my car, not only because it was mine, but because he hadn't driven me anywhere in such a long time, not since we were teenagers and he'd had his license before I did. He was a good driver then, cautious, defensive, and I doubted whether that had changed.

Desmond eased his foot off the brake, and the car crept forward, the knife rocking on the dash. There was a delivery truck in front of us. A sign in its rear window read, "Drivers Wanted." Beneath that it said, "No Experience Necessary." A phone number was listed at the bottom. I tried memorizing it. There were jobs out there, I knew there were. You just have to keep your eyes peeled, I told myself. Something will come along.

Adult Books

FRANKLIN LANDRY had a strong and even sense of the world, though in sixty-three years, he hadn't seen how that had helped him. He wasn't easily surprised–life in general had ceased to shock him–but when his landlord knocked on his door and asked him for advice, Franklin was dumbfounded. In the seven years he'd lived in the small apartment complex, the most Reggie had ever wanted from him was the time. So when he said he needed help with his son, some friendly guidance, Franklin pretended like he hadn't heard him, forcing Reggie to repeat himself. That way Franklin could be sure his ears weren't deceiving him.

"My boy, Victor," Reggie said, restating his plight. "I don't know what to do about him. He says he wants to be a professional photographer. Says he wants to do those artsy kind of nudes."

From what Franklin knew of Victor, he thought artsy nudes probably meant pictures of naked girls on the hoods of cars. Reggie had let his son move into the apartment below Franklin's, rent-free, when he started at the local community college, and Franklin could tell that the boy rarely went to class. Whenever Victor was home, the smell of burned pizza and the screeching sound of guitar music drifted up through the heating vents. Franklin would have complained if Victor wasn't Reggie's son. Instead, he plugged his ears with cotton and tried to ignore it when his floorboards shook from the noise.

"Victor's never even owned a camera," Reggie exclaimed.

He had propped himself in the doorway to Franklin's apartment and, as he spoke, he spun his car keys around his finger casually. The rent was overdue, and Reggie was really there to collect. Luckily, Franklin had managed to scrape the money together at the last minute, paying two dollars of it in change. His Social Security didn't go far, and the pension he drew was small. Stretching his checks over each month was like trying to cover himself with a pillowcase instead of a blanket. He did some maintenance around the building, took care of the lawn, and plunged the occasional toilet, and for that Reggie lowered his rent. Still, Franklin was struggling. He had actually planned on asking for some extra work before Reggie brought up his son.

"Since he doesn't have any experience in photography," Reggie went on, "he's thought of a way to get his foot in the door. He's going to write stories, sexy stories, and send them into, well, *those* kinds of magazines. Then he'll know somebody there, and they can help him. He'll be making contacts, you see."

This was, possibly, the stupidest idea Franklin had ever heard. But he had no intention of telling Reggie that. He couldn't take any chances.

"Contacts, you say?"

Reggie nodded enthusiastically. "He's already written one story. It's about cantaloupes and carrots and whatnot, instead of the real words. Sort of hinting at stuff. That's Victor's angle. You know, talking *around* the subject." Reggie tipped his head back proudly, then amended his expression to that of a disapproving parent. "But all the same, that's not right what he's doing. It's no career."

"Vegetables, huh?" Franklin said, acting impressed.

"Wait. There's more to it. Victor's taken a job at this, well, adult bookstore. Says it's a way of getting started. Bottom of the ladder type of thing."

Franklin couldn't help himself. "Let me get this straight. He's working at a porno shop so he can be a photographer?"

Reggie bristled. "It's called the Pleasure Palace. To be precise. They sell . . . specialty items."

Franklin didn't have any children, but he could see why Reggie wouldn't want his boy clerking at any place with the words *pleasure* and *palace* in the title. It wasn't the sort of position you'd be real anxious to tell the neighbors about. Reggie clearly wasn't overjoyed with Victor's choice of occupation, yet he seemed to want to believe that the kid was finally getting his act together. Franklin had heard that Victor had run away a few times while he was growing up. To keep him around, Reggie bought him things: the high-powered stereo, clothes, an expensive set of golf clubs. He had even leased him a new car, which Victor promptly crashed into a light pole while tuning the radio. Nevertheless, Reggie was allowing the boy to keep the car and was also footing the bill for the repairs. It seemed to Franklin that Reggie was constantly tiptoeing around his son, as if he had to be careful not to upset him, so it was no wonder he had let the cost of the crumpled fender slide.

"I really don't know what to tell you, Reg."

"I thought maybe you could talk to him."

"Hell, why me?"

"He likes you, Franklin. Always has. Heck, he respects you."

This was, without question, a complete lie, and from the way Reggie said it, Franklin sensed that he'd chosen his words ahead of time. Franklin couldn't decide whether to be mad at the guy for trying to butter him up or to feel bad for him. He must have been desperate if he was willing to stoop to flattery.

"What do you want me to do, Reg? Offer to let him use my Polaroid?"

"No," Reggie chuckled. "Tell him about your old job and what that was like."

"Don't see how much good that'll do."

Franklin had spent the better part of his life working at a factory that made cardboard boxes, a fact that would be of little interest to Victor.

"Franklin, buddy," Reggie intoned, still twirling his keys. "All I'm asking is for you to explain to him what his options are."

As usual, Reggie was about as subtle as a foghorn. A blind man could have read between the lines of what he was asking. He wanted Franklin to do his dirty work, to talk Victor out of all that nonsense about the photography and the adult bookstore.

"Say," Reggie said, "I meant to tell you that I'm thinking of having the hallways repainted. They're due." He pretended to pick at a chip outside Franklin's door. "The paint won't cost much, but hiring someone to do the labor will." Reggie looked at him hopefully.

This wasn't a bribe, it was more like a stranglehold. Franklin considered slamming the door in Reggie's face, but the money he'd earn for painting the hallways would easily see him through the next couple of months.

Franklin sighed. "Victor's in apartment C, right?" he asked, though he didn't need to be told.

"Yes, sir. One floor down, directly beneath yours," Reggie answered, beaming. "He's right here under your feet."

THE NEXT DAY, Franklin trudged down to Victor's apartment and knocked on the door. The high, machinelike grind of guitars was rattling the hinges. He knocked once again, assuming the boy hadn't heard him over the noise, and was about to try a third time when Victor finally answered. The door swung open and released a staggering wave of heat that made Franklin squint. The thermostat must have been cranked all the way up. Victor appeared in the doorway wearing a fluorescent tank top and a pair of shorts, as if he were on his way to the beach.

"Can I help you?" Victor yawned.

"Your father told me to, uh, take a look at your bathroom faucet. Said you were having problems. With the faucet, that is."

"No. It's fine. I mean, the water comes out."

Franklin glanced down at the toolbox he'd brought with him but didn't move. If he stood there long enough, he figured that Victor would have to let him in.

"Go ahead." Annoyed, the boy waved him in. "Be my guest."

Inside the apartment, the music was so loud that it made Franklin's muscles vibrate. The heat could have melted a candle. The boy's living room was a mess of dirty dishes and junk, decorated only by a couch, a monstrous pair of speakers, and one poster of a *Playboy* centerfold. Franklin made a beeline for the bathroom, pausing only briefly to note the dozen or so magazines with women on the covers that were piled on the floor.

It was quieter in the bathroom and cooler, but not much. Victor's wet socks were draped over the shower curtain rod. A towel lay beside the toilet in a heap. Franklin closed the door slightly, took out a wrench, and opened the sink cabinet so it would seem like he was working. Victor lowered the music, then Franklin heard him drop onto the couch.

"I see you're a *Playboy* man," Franklin shouted, uncomfortable in the echo off the tiles.

"What?" Victor called back.

"Your poster. I was always a *Penthouse* man myself." He had never been either, never considered the matter at all, but he needed an in.

"Oh. Yeah. I guess," Victor said cautiously.

"Some people say they read those magazines for the articles, but not me." Franklin tapped the wrench against the drainpipe to make it sound as though he was fixing it. "Those people are probably lying, don't you think?"

"Maybe. Who knows?"

He waited for Victor to say more, but the boy didn't go any further. Franklin tried again. "You ever read the articles? They any good?"

"Some are."

"I bet it must be tough to write something to go in between those pictures, to keep the reader interested, if you take my meaning." Franklin leaned heavily against the sink. There was a tube of hair gel sitting on the soap dish instead of soap. The mirror was speckled with water spots. He caught a glimpse of himself and turned away.

"It's not that hard," Victor said. "At least, I don't think it is."

That was all Franklin needed to hear. He tossed the wrench into his toolbox and closed the cabinet.

"All finished in there," he said, stepping out of the bathroom. Then the heat hit him again, hard, solid, airless. He put the box down and wiped his hands on his pants. Victor was sprawled across the couch tossing a ball in the air. "Did you say you wrote for those magazines? Wow. That's impressive."

"No, I meant that I've written stories for them, but I haven't been published or anything."

"Yeah, but writing the story is the first step." Franklin could feel the sweat crawling down his back and trickling over his temples. "Hey, maybe you'll be a famous writer one day, and then I can say I knew you." His shoulders tightened as he resisted a cringe.

"I don't know about that." Victor was thumbing a stain on his shorts. "I'm thinking I want to be a photographer."

"Photography's good."

"But I like to write. I could do a book."

This was it, this was his chance. But Franklin couldn't bring himself to ask the boy about his job. The whole thing had been far more difficult than Franklin had imagined. The noise had rattled his nerves, and the heat had sapped his energy. Now he didn't have the stamina to launch into the speech he'd prepared about making an honest, respectable living.

There was an awkward silence. Franklin finally picked up his toolbox. It seemed heavier than before. "Is it a little hot in here?" he asked, making his way across the boy's littered living room. "It feels hot."

He turned around to find Victor hard on his heels, practically pushing him out into the hallway.

"Nope," Victor said, reaching for the chain lock. "Feels fine to me."

The boy slammed the door, then Franklin found himself

alone in the hall, listening as the sound of the stereo returned, the volume even higher than before.

FRANKLIN TOOK the bus into town. He had sold his car a year earlier to live off the money. Now the bus was his only means of transportation. All of the drivers knew him and would wave him through before he had time to show them his monthly pass. He always flashed it anyway. The pass was about the only thing in his wallet besides his useless driver's license and a picture of his wife. He kept her photograph with him like it was a winning lottery ticket, proof that he had been lucky—that once, he'd had something. She had left him years ago, and he'd gotten used to her absence the same way he'd gotten used to riding the bus. The difference between driving his own car and taking the bus, like having a wife then not having one, wasn't simply a matter of logistics. It was more of a feeling that he had taken so much for granted.

Sometimes Franklin would stay on the bus for hours, circling the city and gazing out the window. He had memorized every house and business on each route, as well as the number of trees and fire hydrants there were on each street. Somehow it comforted him to know that when it came to these few things, he would notice a change immediately.

Franklin got off at the bus stop closest to the Pleasure Palace. The night before, he'd gone through the phone book looking for the address and torn it out. He patted the pocket where he had tucked the scrap of paper, vaguely hoping he had forgotten it, though he knew he hadn't.

It had been two days since the fiasco in Victor's apartment. Franklin wasn't sure if the boy would be working and wasn't eager to find out. He worried that he might fall into a lecture about pornography or that he'd start ranting about the kid's backward schemes. Dread needled him like a rock in his shoe. If he said the wrong thing, Reggie's plan could backfire, and Victor might glue himself to the idea of working at the bookstore. Then there would be no painting job and no money for Franklin.

The Pleasure Palace, it turned out, was not easy to find. Franklin wasn't sure if that was a good omen or a bad one. The one sign marking the store's entrance was a small red plaque by a doorbell at the side of a laundromat. He had expected to see a few men in trench coats and dark glasses skulking around outside the door. Instead, all he found was a potted plant that had been set out to catch the sun.

Franklin peered up at the building, but couldn't see into any of the windows. The image of the centerfold in Victor's apartment fluttered in Franklin's mind. Reggie would come around soon to ask how things went with his son, might even bring a few cans of paint with him as a reminder. In spite of himself and the money, Franklin was too embarrassed to go inside.

He returned to the bus stop in time to see his bus pulling away. Franklin had committed the timetable to memory and knew that the next bus wouldn't be along for awhile. He took a seat on a nearby bench, resigned to the wait and to the fact that his life now ran according to somebody else's schedule.

IN THE MORNING, Franklin found a note under his door. "Please mow the lawn today." Reggie's handwriting. The grass didn't need to be cut. Franklin had done it a few days ago. He couldn't be sure what Reggie was up to, but he'd soon find out. He pictured Reggie sneaking up to his door and quietly sliding the note through the crack. Reggie knew better than to call; Franklin was almost always home, and then he would have had to explain the unnecessary request. While he was down on one knee picking up the note, Franklin thought that his wife would have been astonished if she knew how often he stayed at home. He had been, in her words, a ghost of a ghost in their house. In his mind, he was never away that often, but then he could also remember coming home once and asking her if she'd redecorated, only to be told that nothing was different.

During his marriage, Franklin had convinced himself that the reason he worked such long hours was for the money. All of his overtime, spent practically alone in a warehouse with thousands of flat, unassembled boxes, was for his wife, so he could buy her anything she desired. But she had never asked for much. What she truly wanted was for them to spend more time together. Only after she was gone could Franklin see how afraid he had been of disappointing her, of doing the wrong thing. And that was exactly what he had done. It was a deep, shapeless fear that had ruined him, one he still felt the remnants of, like an old break in his bones.

His wife had left him with little warning. His one hint came when she served him what was to be their last meal on their wedding china. She had picked the pattern out specially, one she'd fallen in love with in a catalog, but they never ate on it. She rarely even took the pieces out of the cabinet, and then it was just to dust them.

Franklin reread the note Reggie had left him. He stood up and squeezed his knee, letting the blood rush back into his leg. Then he reminded himself that one of his dearest memories was of his wife standing in front of the cabinet and staring at the set of dishes, admiring them as though they weren't hers. He had always thought she was silly not to have used the lovely china more often.

THAT AFTERNOON, he dragged the lawn mower out of the basement and refilled the gas tank. He was finishing the strip of grass between the sidewalk and the street when Reggie pulled up in his car.

"I see you got my message," Reggie shouted, leaning over to the passenger side window.

"Yup." Franklin left the lawn mower running on purpose.

"Hope you're wearing a good pair of shoes."

"Pardon?"

"Your shoes. When I was a kid, my uncle cut off eight of his toes mowing the lawn. He was wearing rubber sandals."

"That so?" Franklin said, unimpressed.

"True story," Reggie said. He was fidgeting with the door handle, and Franklin could tell that he was winding up for another one of his pitches.

"So I wanted to ask you–"

"What?" Franklin tapped his ear, acting as if he couldn't hear him over the lawn mower. He wasn't going to let Reggie off lightly.

"My boy, did you talk to him? About your job," he added.

"I'm going to get around to that. I've been pretty busy." This lie rang as falsely as Reggie's one about Victor respecting him.

"Well, I was only stopping by," Reggie retorted. "On my way to the paint store, that is. I'm going to get a few cans to do those halls with. Butter yellow, I think. Or ecru. I don't know which yet."

"So you were just *stopping by?*"

"And I came to get Victor. His car's not ready, and he needs a ride into town." Reggie beeped the horn like he was suddenly in a hurry. "Boy's going to have to start taking the bus, I suppose. Be good for him. See how real folks get around."

Reggie realized his mistake and cleared his throat nervously.

"Well, I guess I'll let you get back to the lawn, Franklin."

"Thanks for stopping by, Reg," Franklin said and resumed his mowing.

Moments later Victor hurried out of the building and climbed into his father's car, pretending like he didn't see Franklin. When Franklin heard the car door shut, he peeked over his shoulder. Both Reggie and Victor were staring at him as they drove away, but neither realized what the other was doing.

FRANKLIN RETURNED to the Pleasure Palace the following afternoon, resolved to go in and talk Victor out of his job. This time the plant was gone. A note taped to the doorbell said that it didn't work and that customers should go straight up to the third floor during business hours. Franklin took a deep breath and stepped up to the door like he was about to jump out of an airplane.

After two flights of stairs, he was winded. He huffed and gulped air as he walked down a dingy hallway to the door marked "The Pleasure Palace." The name, Franklin quickly decided, was far from apt. The store's sign was glued to a clouded glass window that had chicken wire embedded in it. Not quite the door to a palace, he thought. Once inside, he found that the store itself was hardly palatial either. Franklin thought it looked like a cross between a toy store and a Christian Science reading room. One wall was covered with books and magazines. The others held racks of lotions and brightly colored gadgets. He half-expected to see some stuffed animals or a picture of Christ on the wall.

To Franklin's surprise, a woman was seated behind the tall counter in the far corner of the room. She was reading a paperback romance. She didn't even seem to notice that he had come in. In an effort to act like he was browsing, Franklin took a small box off one of the shelves. Once he saw the word *anal* printed on the lid, he put it back. Any curiosity he'd had about stores like this one dwindled the instant he remembered why he was there.

Franklin mustered his courage and approached the counter. "Excuse me, Miss," he said. "Could you tell me if Victor is working today?"

The clerk raised her head slowly, as though physically pulling herself out of the story. She was heavy and older than Franklin thought she would be.

"Nobody named Victor works here," she said, like that should have somehow been obvious to him.

"He doesn't. Are you sure?"

"I'm sure," the clerk answered. Her hair hung over her eyes and moved when she blinked.

"You're absolutely positive that nobody named Victor works here?" Franklin asked, utterly confused. His eyes landed on a row of clear packages full of inflatable men and women, the faces pressed flat against the plastic. "I was supposed to talk to him."

"He doesn't work here."

"I know this sounds strange, but someone told me that he

worked here, and they asked me to come and speak with him."
Franklin thought he must have been blushing. He didn't understand why Reggie would send him on a wild goose chase. He couldn't figure out what was going on.

Now the clerk was getting annoyed. "Like I said, he doesn't work here. I'd know."

"I'm sorry," Franklin said, trying to lighten the situation. "You probably hear a lot of strange stuff from the guys who come into this place."

"It's not just the men. Trust me. It's the women too. Everybody wants to talk," the clerk said, resting her head on her hand. It sounded as if she was repeating a speech. "Either they're nervous or they're bored or they're freaks. Not like deviant freaks, but no-social-skills types. And I'm always like, 'Look, if I wanted to listen to your life story, I would have been a bartender or a priest.'"

Franklin was stuck on the part about women coming into the store. He couldn't visualize it. "Really, you get a lot of ladies shopping in here?"

"Of course," she said, bothered by the question. "This one woman came in about an hour before you. She'd just left her husband. Walked out on him. Told me her bags were in her trunk. She bought a magazine and said she wanted to see a real man for a change. I said, 'Whatever.'"

Franklin thought of his wife, transposing her face onto an image of a woman storming into the store and slapping a magazine down on the counter.

"People do strange shit," the clerk said. "You only have to be on this earth ten minutes to know that."

Franklin wanted the clerk to notice the effect her story had had on him, to magically see what he had imagined, and tell him that he was wrong, that the woman was nothing like his wife. He wanted her to tell him to forget about it.

"You know what I mean?" she said.

"Yeah. Sure," he mumbled, and walked out without closing the door behind him.

THE NEXT DAY, Franklin found himself riding the bus around the city. It was clear to him which houses had recently replanted their flower beds and which buildings had reshingled their roofs. Each time he spotted something new, he had to remind himself not to remark on it to the person in the seat next to him.

He was trying to figure out why Reggie had set him up like that, but his thoughts kept returning to his wife. Franklin often wondered what her life was like now, if she was happy. He liked to think that she was better off without him. That way he could believe he had done her a favor, that in a sense he had done right by her. That was all he'd ever wanted to do in the first place.

The image of the lady in the store was like a cramp in Franklin's side. He felt a pressing need to ask the clerk what else she remembered about her. Whatever she could recall, he wanted to know.

Like the last time, the stairs up to the store were hard on him. Franklin had to rest at the top and catch his breath before going in. When he entered, the clerk was in the same position, huddled over a book on her stool, as if she'd never moved. And again, she did not acknowledge his arrival.

"Hello," Franklin said brightly, but a little short of air. "It's me. Remember?"

The woman set down her paperback, a different one than the previous day. It took her a second to place him. "Oh. Yeah. You," she said, unfazed.

A mug with ceramic breasts on it was sitting by the register, steaming with black coffee. "Nice cup," Franklin said. An anxious attempt at levity. The woman didn't even crack a smile.

"I wanted to ask you," he began. "The lady you told me about, the one who came in after she left her husband, what was she like? What I mean is, was she sad? Was she angry? How'd she look?"

Without changing her expression, the clerk said, "Listen, we're all about privacy here. No names, no numbers, no referrals."

82

"No, you don't understand. I don't want to call her. I'm only trying to find out if she was happier after she left her husband, if she seemed all right."

"Okay, remember we talked about freaks last time you were here, like social second-graders, well you're on the verge now. You're skating into the am-I-going-to-have-to-call-the-cops zone."

"That's not what I . . ." Franklin couldn't finish his sentence. He eased away from her. The clerk took a sip of coffee from the mug and leafed through the pages of her paperback, trying to get back to her place. Then Franklin left, careful to shut the door behind him.

REGGIE WAS standing in front of his apartment when Franklin returned home.

"Glad I ran into you," Reggie said, a piece of paper in his hand. "I was about to leave you a message about not burning the leaves from the lawn."

Franklin considered taking a swing at Reggie for playing the joke on him, but he held back. He decided to wait and see if Reggie would mention the Pleasure Palace on his own.

"Burning leaves is illegal, Reg."

"That's what I wrote." He showed the note to Franklin. It said, "Please don't burn leaves. It's illegal." Then he wadded up the paper and stuffed it into his pocket. Reggie was wearing a suit, and the ball of paper bulged through his trousers.

Franklin eyed his outfit. "What's with the suit? You going to traffic court today?"

"No, no, the car dealership. To see how they're getting along with Victor's car. I wear this suit to let them know I'm not some jerk they can push around. You know what I mean?"

The comment stung Franklin, more than he thought it could. He took out his keys and put them in the lock.

"Victor told me he wrote another one, another story," Reggie blurted. "And that he's going to start sending them around. See if any of the fish bite. So I was wondering, did you get a chance to go over to the, uh, to talk to him?"

Franklin felt humiliation spread over his skin like a sunburn. Reggie had strung him along, and he'd taken the bait. He had no idea why Reggie had done it, but Franklin wasn't about to give him the satisfaction of knowing how far he had gone for the money. Franklin shook his head solemnly, acting as if he hadn't spoken to Victor at all.

"Well, you're going to do it soon, right? We don't have all the time in the world here."

These were probably the same lines Reggie was going to use on the guys at the dealership, Franklin thought.

"Right?" Reggie asked.

Franklin opened his front door. Reggie was clenching his fist around the paper in his pocket. Flushed and panting, he looked the way Franklin pictured himself looking after a couple of flights of stairs.

"Okay, Franklin. I get the picture. Thanks. Thanks a lot, buddy," Reggie said, stalking away. Halfway down the hall, he shouted, "Oh and, for your information, the painters will start next week."

With that, Reggie disappeared into the stairwell, pounding down the steps. Reggie's voice was still ringing between the walls with their cracking paint. The words resounded in Franklin's mind until he could no longer distinguish if it was the echo in the empty corridor or not.

FRANKLIN LAY on his couch until the urge to go back and apologize to the clerk at the Pleasure Palace made it impossible to sleep or concentrate.

When he caught the bus, the driver, an older man he'd never seen before, asked him for his pass.

"You new?" Franklin asked, opening his wallet. A cool October wind was blowing in from outside, and he could feel it through his coat.

"Today's my first day," the man said sternly, closing the doors with the pull of a lever. "I thought I was retired. I guess I was wrong."

By the time the bus arrived at the stop by the Pleasure

Palace, Franklin had realized that there would be little point in trying to excuse himself to the woman. It didn't matter to her who he was or what he did, as long as he didn't do it around her. He closed his eyes until he heard the doors fold shut.

When he opened them, Victor was standing by the driver, counting his coins. "Exact change only. That's the rule," the driver was saying.

Franklin jumped up, fumbling for his wallet, and cut to the front of the bus.

"I'll pay," he said. "This boy's with me."

The man frowned. "I don't think I can let two people go on the same pass."

"Sure you can," Franklin lied, guiding Victor to the back of the bus with him. "Didn't they tell you that?"

Victor plopped down in a seat by the window, the zipper on his jacket scraping over the plastic. "Thanks," he said self-consciously. "I don't take the bus, like, ever. My car's in the shop."

Franklin nodded, then neither spoke for awhile.

"Tell me something?" Franklin finally asked. "Why does your father think you work at the Pleasure Palace?"

"Oh God." Victor rolled his eyes. "Man, I just told him that to make him feel better."

"To make him feel *better?*"

"My dad always thinks I'm going to take off and run away again. I made up that stuff about photography and writing so he'd think I was all serious about a career. To get him off my back, you know. I thought he sent you in to grill me, so I told you the same story. I only said I worked at the Pleasure Palace because it's this nasty old place where losers go to buy porn. I didn't think he'd ever go there to check if I was lying."

Franklin sat back. "What about the poster and the magazines in your apartment?"

"Don't get me wrong, Mr. Landry, I like women. But I don't read the articles between the pictures. Nobody does."

"Why didn't you explain all of this to your father?"

"I don't know. Next month I'll say I want to do something else, some normal shit like insurance."

Now Franklin understood. In trying to spare his father one heartache, Victor had given him another. Franklin considered explaining to Victor the side effects of his gesture, but he decided that it wasn't worth it. They wouldn't matter to the boy, because he thought he was doing the right thing. Franklin knew that feeling.

"You're not going to tell him, are you, about what I said?" Victor asked.

Franklin shook his head. He hadn't put his wallet away, and he became aware of how light it was as it lay in his palm.

"Hey," Victor said, wiping the condensation from the window. "Is this the bus we're supposed to be on? It seems like we're headed in the wrong direction. This doesn't look like the way to get to our building."

Franklin was picturing the men who would come to paint the hallways, the drop cloths on the floor and the rolling pans, the sharp smell of turpentine seeping under his door.

"This is the right one," Franklin told him. "We're fine," he said as the houses and lawns and cars flashed by outside, then blurred as they met the foggy edge of the glass the boy had cleared.

A Decent Night's Sleep

I HADN'T AGREED to anything, but by then, that was beside the point.

We were in Venice, staying in a hotel that had seen better days. Me in one room, my mother and her new husband Edgar in the other. Their room had a television and a view of the canal. Mine, a converted closet, was just big enough to hold a single bed. It was dark and smelled of wilted flowers, and the thin mattress was covered only in a rubber sheet. A hollow door connected our two rooms, which made me wonder if my mother had intentionally said the reservation was for her *daughter*, rather than an adult, a grown woman. At the time, she had probably wanted me nearby, to keep me within earshot, but since we'd arrived she'd been ignoring me and likely regretting how close we were going to have to be.

"Could you open the window in there?" I called. I wanted to get a little cross-ventilation to draw out the smell. There was no response.

Since the incident in the lobby that morning, my mother had said little, and I'd barely spoken except to ask Edgar to help me with my luggage. He was a thin man, and he was tan and muscular in a way that I didn't think someone his age could be. He unpacked while my mother lay in bed, carrying on as though the jet lag had really gotten to her. She was acting like coming to Venice wasn't her idea in the first place, and I suspected that the performance was to prove to me how much I'd hurt her, that she could be hurt.

I poked my head into their room. "Did you say something?" Edgar asked.

"The window," I said. "I wanted to open it."

"It's all yours," he chimed and set a suitcase down beside my mother's feet.

She had come to Venice to study Renaissance painting with a college tour group, and Edgar, who had recently retired from his job as a claims adjuster–decades of assessing people's damaged lives–had planned on relaxing, sleeping late, and seeing a few big sights. I'd joined them at the last minute and, though he tried not to show it, Edgar did not appreciate the sudden change of plans. My mother had begged me to come and had even reserved an airline ticket to force my hand. The only reason I showed up at the airport was out of fear that she'd waste her vacation worrying about me if I wasn't there. Considering the situation, I felt sorry for Edgar. He'd never had any say in the matter either.

"Forget the window, darling," my mother said. "We have to get ready. We have to leave."

She was supposed to meet her group for the first day of a four-day seminar within the hour. Neither Edgar nor I would be attending, but she wanted us to see her to the church where the first lecture was being held.

Edgar checked his watch. "Then let's shake a leg," he said, slipping on a safari-style vest over his pastel shirt.

Sometimes it seemed like that was the only type of thing he knew how to say, fast clichés and peppy retorts. For an instant, Edgar reminded me of someone who would try to sell you a watch out of their briefcase. In reality, he was just the opposite. He took vitamins and sent people birthday cards. He played backgammon and subscribed to woodworking magazines. Edgar had even started calling me darling, as was my mother's habit. At first, I thought it was because he'd forgotten my name, but I found out later that he had begun to address all of his children in the same way. They were grown too, some older than me, with children of their own, and months earlier I had been introduced to all of them at my husband's funeral. That was when I heard Edgar say it. "Darling," he had whispered to each of them in turn. "See if Judith needs anything. See what she needs." As I stood across from him in the dim hotel room, I found that I could only fault Edgar for being eager and aggressively nice.

"He's right, darling. I don't want to be late," my mother said. She sat up and groped for her shoes under the bed, then turned to me. "What are you waiting for?"

WHILE EDGAR was in the bathroom, my mother asked me to let him pick a place for us to visit that day.

"If he wants to go to the Rialto Bridge and look at the plastic Leaning Towers of Pisa, try and act interested. Okay?"

"I thought he was on vacation," I said. "I thought that the only thing he wanted to do was nap and read the paper."

Before we'd left, my mother had made a point of telling me how much time I would have to myself. She'd practically guaranteed it, and that was the one thing that would make the trip bearable. Since Douglas's death, friends had made it their job to be strong for me, to put on a good face, but I had to punch their time cards, let them know it was working. I had been pulling double duty, and I just wanted to be alone for awhile.

"No, darling," my mother said, fixing her make-up in the mirror. "He wants to be with you. Tour the city together."

This was such a blatant lie that I couldn't believe she said it without flinching. Her attempt at enthusiasm was transparent; what made it worse was that it was clearly for my benefit. The whole trip was. People had been going out of their way for me for so long that instead of making me feel better, it made me sick. I felt like crying, but I didn't want to scare my mother. She was finishing with her make-up, and I could see that her blush, though carefully applied, was too bright and would probably look like the trail of a comet in the daylight. I decided not to tell her.

EDGAR AND I walked my mother through the maze of narrow, dusky lanes and tiny bridges to the back of the church of Santa Maria Gloriosa, a squat and stocky brick building that, from the outside, had the quaint charm of a barn rather than the grandeur of a church. Once there, she told us we didn't have to see her to the door. The group would be waiting, she said, and she would be fine. We made plans to meet her a few hours later at the Piazza San Marco, then she kissed both of us breezily on each cheek and quickly rounded the corner, slipping out of sight.

Edgar hesitated for a minute, watching her go. "If your mother had kissed me like that again, I think I would have gotten motion sickness." He was hurt by the way she had hurried off. But it wasn't any teenage-type embarrassment at being seen with her family that had sent her running. It was probably panic. Leaving Edgar and I alone together was a bad idea at best and, like a pickpocket, she'd disappeared into the city before anyone had time to realize what she had done.

My husband's death had changed my mother. It had turned her into a mother again, only she wasn't acting like I was her daughter. She took up the objective distance of a family friend, one who had been acquainted with such tragedies because she was someone else's mother, had nursed another child through their pain. "Grief," she announced, weeks after the funeral, "is like vomit. You don't want to keep it inside you. I heard that on the television."

To her, the fact that I still had little appetite and hadn't slept through a whole night in ages were sure signs that I needed her brand of therapy, a sort of shock treatment that meant diving back into the world headfirst. The details of Douglas's death seemed to confirm that.

He had died in a manner usually reserved for people on soap operas. Within a week of being diagnosed with an inalterably fatal disease, he had been buried. His death wasn't drawn out, so, the way my mother saw it, why prolong his mourning? Which implied that I was the one who was being melodramatic. "It's not a secret," she had said. "You hide in your house, acting like no one knows. Remember, darling, there were guests at the funeral. People know."

I wasn't trying to keep Douglas's death quiet. What I wanted to avoid was the steady stream of advice that flowed in with each visitor and condolence card. The flowers from my co-workers at the bank came with inspirational poems. A letter from Douglas's old tennis partner included a psychologist's business card. After a while, the gifts stopped coming and everyone's two cents turned into a dismaying mountain of spare change. By taking me on the trip with her, my mother was bypassing prescriptions for a cure. However, I wasn't prepared for what her method of recovery would entail.

While we were checking into the hotel, she pointed at my shirt and asked, "Did you have to wear that?"

I had unconsciously chosen a black silk shirt to travel in. This was a signal to my mother that I was holding back, that I wasn't with her one hundred percent. My reaction to her question was stunning, even to me. "As I recall, you wore black too every time you lost a husband," I said, my voice rising. "Only none of them were dead."

The lobby, which was full of Indian senior citizens just off a tour boat, was marble, and my words seemed to ricochet between the floors and walls and around the people. The smell of burned coffee left over from the continental breakfast was, I imagined, the scent of what I'd said singeing the air. My mother's face was frozen in recognition. My father had left her when I was a girl, and she had married and divorced her second husband during the years I was away at college. Loss was a concept she understood, but not in the permanent sense. She walked away from me instantly, following the bellman to our room, and left Edgar to finish at the desk.

"I can handle this," he had said, meaning I should follow her and try to make up. He loved my mother, not in a passionate way, but sincerely. He wanted to take care of her. Edgar had quietly supported all of her attempts to get me to snap back, but never said anything to me directly. While my mother badgered and pleaded, citing the words of advice columnists and talk show hosts, Edgar simply nodded in tacit agreement. He was like that, satisfied to sit on the sidelines of life and watch. It was hard to believe they got along or could even hold a conversation, but by that time, the question of compatibility was beyond asking.

THE SUN moved behind a cloud, casting the back of the church into shadow, and Edgar looked up. "I guess that's a hint that we should get going."

He pulled a packet of maps and brochures my mother had given him from inside his vest and began flipping though them. "The majestic city of islands, blah, blah. The palace of this, *piazetta* of that," he said, running his finger over the guides as though scouring them.

"Look," he said, replacing the packet. "Let's just wing it. Let's be Ugly Americans and stroll around and stare at everything like it's a traffic accident. How's that sound?"

"Great," I managed to say, though this was probably the worst idea he could have had. Granted, Edgar wasn't wearing black socks, sandals, and a flowered shirt, but there could be no mistaking him. I had hoped to get him into a museum, preferably on a guided tour, where everyone's behavior would follow a certain mode and, most importantly, talking would not be encouraged.

He zipped his vest briskly, indicating he was ready for whatever adventure we were about to embark on, and I tried to convince myself that there was more to him than met the eye. I could still picture the self-help guides strewn around his house after the funeral. He'd bought books about death and family situations like ours, ones with catchy titles, usually double entendres, and left them out in noticeable places until he assumed I must have seen them. My guess was that he saw our vacation as his opportunity to try out all of the tactics and strategies that his books had recommended, which made me feel like each day was going to be devoted to a different maneuver. The books actually used words like those, expressly military and combative. The language, I realized, said more about our relationship than either of us could.

I followed Edgar to a water bus docked nearby. He had decided that sightseeing by boat would be easier on our feet. When we got on board, he paid our fares with a hundred thousand lire note. The woman who took the money sized him up, then said, in heavily accented English, "Welcome to Venice," and handed him a stack of bills.

Once we were on the Grand Canal, the city changed perspective. The buildings looked like a shelf of weathered, random books, and the barber-striped poles that the gondolas were tied to made it appear as though the whole city was already half sunken and not really floating at all.

After nearly an hour on board, Edgar suggested we get off. We were approaching the next stop, and I noticed that there was a crowd formed around a fountain by the dock. To Edgar, that must have been as good an invitation as any.

The people were gathered to watch a bony, almost naked man contort himself into a clear plastic box. His arms were twisted and knotted behind his back, and he had curled his legs unnervingly around his head. With a jerk, his whole body was flush in the box, then a girl ran over and shut the lid. She left him inside and darted around the crowd, holding out a basket for money.

As Edgar affected a quick search of his vest, I found myself marveling at how strange and pitiful the whole scene was, including Edgar. A week before Douglas had died, I came home to find the living room couch burning on the front lawn. Douglas was standing beside it. He told me that he hated the couch, that it was old and tacky, and that he wouldn't be able to rest in peace if I kept it. At that point, he knew it was only a matter of days. "This was a mercy killing," he'd said, then left me to beat out the flames with a rubber floor mat from the car. In the end, all that remained was a smoldering row of springs and the frame, which had become unrecognizable. Like the couch, Edgar was not specifically the problem, but he seemed to embody all that was wrong with the world, all that was cheap and tasteless but inescapably real.

"Come on, " Edgar said, tugging my shirt lightly. "Show's over."

As we wandered through the winding alleys, I kept letting myself fall behind Edgar, then I would wait to see how long it took him to come back around or to let me catch up. It was as if I could measure how bored he was in minutes. When we were together, we walked silently, each pretending to be fascinated or at least interested in the ruined walls and crumbling water stairs. It was late in the afternoon, and my mother wouldn't be meeting us for another two hours.

"Is there anything special you want to do?" Edgar asked. He put his arms over his head and stretched.

I couldn't think of one thing. Every item on the list of possibilities was equally unpleasant because we would have to do it together. Looking up, past the tall, tight rows of buildings, I felt like I was at the bottom of a well. The sky, which was a uniformly dull blue, was only visible between the balconies and awnings. The smell of the canals, a dank bitterness, made the impression more intense. I had come to feel Douglas's death in different ways, and sometimes it was like this, just a sensation. Often, though, it was physical—blurred vision or muscle cramps in my hands that froze my fingers into fists. Other times, it was as if someone kept kicking my feet out from under me. Because I couldn't anticipate how it would hit me, each day felt like walking into a strange, dark room. I never knew what was waiting.

I remembered what my mother had asked me back at the hotel. "I'll go wherever you want to go, Edgar. Whatever you want to do, I'll do."

Edgar dropped his arms abruptly, as if my answer was an insult.

"You know, Judith, I think you should start doing what you want, not what other people want. It's your life too. You call the shots." He laced his fingers together to do another stretch, then started off again, compelling me to follow him as he spoke. "You need to reclaim your life. It'll make you feel better," he said.

Edgar was one of the few people who hadn't volunteered his advice, and I should have seen it coming. I'd been told that everything from Valium to karate classes would make me feel better and, like everyone else, he seemed convinced that he knew exactly what I needed. His confidence made my teeth clench. I didn't think I could take much more of him.

While lingering to let Edgar get farther in front of me, I spotted a poster next to a butcher shop. It was for an exhibit of Salvador Dali prints. In the window, beside the poster, a pig's leg was pirouetting on its one intact hoof. The hoof reminded me of Dali's work, and I seized upon the notion that the prints might be disturbing, that Edgar, who couldn't even watch baby animals being born on nature programs, would have trouble with them. They would make him uncomfortable. It was a petty, immature idea, but I couldn't help myself.

I called to him, and he took his time retracing his path. "I'm sorry," Edgar said. "I didn't realize how far you'd gotten behind me. Did you find something for us to do?"

"Well, there's this exhibit. It's Dali. He's famous."

"Oh, Dali," Edgar sung, as though the artist was a personal friend. "I know him. Wasn't he the one who'd starve himself until he hallucinated so he could paint all of those crazy pictures?"

I shrugged and gave him a noncommittal smile.

"Sure," Edgar said, and found the address on his map. "It's not too far. I think I'm up for some melted clocks."

THE EXHIBIT was being held in a gallery at the back of an unremarkable stone building. No one was in line, but the poster I'd seen was tacked to a board out front. Inside, an attendant handed each of us a small metal button to bend around our shirt collars. "Dali" was written on it in purple script. While I slipped mine into my pocket, Edgar hung his crookedly off his vest.

Surprisingly, the aisles between the overlit artwork were full of people, all wearing rigid hiking backpacks and heavy boots. Most were so tall and blatantly blond that I thought they might be a band of Swedish tourists. They were milling around beside one another, just barely avoiding powerful collisions, and pointing at the artwork.

The gallery itself was a mishmash of styles, a slice of every century the city had seen. The archways and stucco walls on which the pieces hung were at odds with the slick black frames and track lighting. The tiled floor was dented and had buckled as though the sea flowed directly beneath it. And something somewhere was dripping. My first impulse was to wrap my arms around myself, to keep warm, but the room wasn't the least bit cold.

Edgar was working his way around the tourists, moving quickly from picture to picture and re-adjusting his expression to coincide with the style of the print. He scowled at the overtly sexual drawings of unicorns and put on a face of mock surprise when he stood before what looked, at first glance, to be a picture of wineglasses but was actually a sketch of nude women. He was apparently at ease there. Even the headless torsos didn't seem to put him off. I soon gave up on my small revenge and said, "We can go if you want to."

"No, no, we can stay."

He was trying so desperately to act cheerful that it occurred to me that my mother had not only asked me to placate Edgar, she had also asked him to do the same for me. She'd played both sides. That would explain why Edgar had agreed to the exhibit in the first place.

"I'm going to see if I can find one I can relate to," Edgar said. "See if he did any sad clowns or kittens in a basket. Don't worry about me. I'll be fine."

I circled the gallery feeling guilty and killing time. Edgar was at the opposite end of the room. He had stopped trying to look at the art and was just glancing around the way someone might if they were waiting for a ride.

When one of the tourists bumped into me, I turned to find that they were all whispering and backing up toward the walls. A gypsy woman, with a dirt-smudged face and soiled clothes, was dragging a boy beside her through the gallery. The boy's arms and legs were so thin and alarmingly twisted that he must have been incapable of walking on his own. One of his arms was thrown over her shoulder and strapped to it with a rope. His eyes and tongue lolled when she moved. She had one hand around his waist and the other was outstretched, holding a Styrofoam cup for change.

Some of the tourists dropped coins into the cup. Others could only stare. The further the woman had to drag the boy, the more aggressive she got, thrusting her cup into people's faces and demanding money in an unrecognizable language.

Edgar had his back to her. He didn't see or hear her approaching. The woman noticed this and headed straight for him with the boy's feet lagging over the tiles. It was as if I were now watching that traffic accident Edgar had mentioned earlier. My voice was caught in my throat. My feet were nailed to the floor. I couldn't warn him.

Oblivious, Edgar stepped backwards and slammed right into them. As if on cue, the woman fell to the floor on top of the boy. All of the tourists were staring at the three of them, and I could not help but drop my eyes.

When I was finally able to look up again, I saw the woman pinching the boy and muttering something to him. With that, he let out a slow, guttural moan that wound down until he was out of breath, then started again.

The woman began shouting incomprehensibly, making a show of the fact that she couldn't pick the boy back up. She shook the cup at Edgar while he tried to help her. When he went to lift the boy, putting his arms beneath him like a baby, the woman knocked the cup against his chest. She made it clear that he wasn't allowed to help the boy until he had given something to her.

Hanging over the scene was a large picture of a disembodied head. Its expression was so deeply blank that it didn't apply to reality. I could see Edgar, the woman, and the boy reflected as a mass in the dark part of the glass above them.

Edgar dug into his vest, then stuffed a pocketful of money into the cup, giving away all he had. Afterwards, the woman let him lean the boy up against her. The attendant who had handed us the buttons cut through the crowd and yelled at the woman in Italian. He grabbed her by the arm and started pulling her toward the door, but she went willingly, satisfied by the wad of money she was folding into her shirt. Then Edgar was left standing alone in the middle of the gallery.

The urge to run to him, to stand in front of him and hide him, swelled in my heart, then faltered. I was caught behind a group of tourists who were now gaping at him in the same way the people at the fountain had gaped at the man in the box. Edgar was only a few yards away from me, but he might as well have been standing in the middle of a highway.

Sound returned to the gallery, a mix of hushed comments and the murmur of moving feet. I finally made my way over to Edgar. I waited behind him for a second, then reached for him, but my fingers only skimmed his vest.

In a low voice, I asked, "Are you all right?"

"Yeah," he said. His eyes, unfocused, swept over me, missing me entirely.

"Let's leave," I told him, touching his wrist. I felt a little dizzy, like I'd just surfaced from swimming the length of a pool. I realized that I had been holding my breath, and now it was an effort to get my balance.

As we made our way back through the gallery, the tourists gazed at us, their faces backlit and in shadow except for their eyes and the tops of their heads. They could all be part of the exhibition, I thought, if they just stayed there and didn't move.

Outside, even the pale sky seemed bright. Edgar went to the edge of the canal, then stood there quietly. I asked him for one of the maps. "So we can figure out how to get to the place where we're supposed to meet my mother."

"Oh. Good. Good thinking." He got the map and handed it to me, but wouldn't let it go.

"Before I met your mother, I ran over a man with my car," Edgar blurted. "I wasn't drunk or anything. I just didn't see him. It sounds sort of funny, like it's the kind of thing that doesn't really happen." He was scuffing at the side of the canal like a child, unwilling to look at me.

"He was the one who was drunk, actually. He was sleeping in the street. When people say that, you don't think they're *in* the street. But this guy was. Kind of on the sidewalk and in the gutter. In the gutter, there's another one. Really, I only ran over his legs," Edgar said, putting up the palms of his hands, as though what he had done was an unfortunate but common occurrence, not unlike getting a flat tire.

"Are you serious?" I asked. "I mean, are you being serious?"

Edgar was shifting his weight from one foot to the other, slowly swaying, and I had to keep myself from reaching out and holding him in place. He scanned the sidewalk like whatever he needed to say next was written somewhere between the pebbles and stones. Here was a man who'd spent his whole life putting other people's grief into succinct files, and he didn't seem to know the lines to his own story. I doubted that he'd ever told it to anyone before.

"On the way to the emergency room the man kept telling

me that he just wanted to get some rest. He said a decent night's sleep was all he needed, but that people kept trying to get him off the street. He didn't scream or cry or anything. When I told him I was sorry and that I didn't see him, he said it was okay, understandable. He said he was going incognito: 'I was making like a curb, so no one would see me.' He asked me how he was supposed to get any sleep after what had happened, then he passed out." Edgar crossed his arms over his stomach.

"After they bandaged him up, his legs still looked flat, and they hung out at the wrong angles. His legs were like that boy's, all loose and weak looking. I got a call later from the hospital. A doctor told me that the man had died, that he'd had some sort of cancer already and that his liver gave out. The doctor said the man had one foot in the grave, and I said, 'Yeah, and I tripped him.' It was a stupid thing to say, considering."

Edgar took the map from my hand and began searching for the way back. "There was stuff with the police, but it all got worked out," he said, his voice lightening. Now it sounded like he was retelling someone else's tale. "Paid for the guy's headstone in the end. We could go see it sometime if you want. Not that you'd want to see another one, but if you're interested."

I thought I ought to say something to Edgar, that I finally could say something to him, the one person who might know a little of what I felt, but he was already on his way to forgetting all that had happened in the past few minutes. The tightness had disappeared from his face, and his expression slid back to its usual ease. He was pretending nothing had gone on and, for that, I was suddenly grateful. Because I didn't want his secret. I had no place to put it. Maybe, I thought, this act was for me, that perhaps Edgar didn't want his story to be the only thing we shared.

He held one side of the map out to me so I could help him keep it open. When I took it, he smiled briefly, as if with my gesture I had agreed that the events of the day would stay between the two of us. He glanced at me again, and I nodded. Not to let him know that the deal was good, though I would never repeat anything he had told me, but to thank him for what I hoped he had done.

IT WAS dusk when we reached the Piazza San Marco, and there were more pigeons than people in the square. We chose one of the many empty tables at the piazza's café and sat there while a pack of waiters stood in the shadows of the trellised arcade, smoking and ignoring us. Eventually, one of them came to our table and gave us two menus, but darted off before we could ask him for a third.

At the other end of the square, a small blond child was running through a flock of pigeons, whirling and coaxing the birds up into the air, only to have them skid back to the ground a few feet from where they left off.

"The waiters are blasé and the birds are blasé," Edgar said, pulling a dyed carnation out of the vase on the table.

Now surrounded by pigeons, the child began to sob. The mother clapped to startle the birds away, but the same thing happened. They scattered and circled, then returned. The sobbing turned into a high, falling wail when the child noticed that one of the pigeons had a torn wing and was left to waddle around, unable to fly.

"Isn't that sad?" Edgar asked, gazing out over the piazza. I wasn't sure if he was talking about the bird or the child or what had gone on that day. Maybe he didn't know, either.

"We need another menu," I said. "My mother should be here soon." Edgar nodded and replaced the flower, arranging it so it was in the same position it had been in before. We took turns scanning the café, but our waiter was nowhere to be found. After awhile, we gave up and sat there listening as the echo of flapping wings steadily filled the square.

When she finally appeared from across the piazza, my mother was waving and calling, "Ciao, mi familia bella." Once she reached the table, she dropped her bags and slumped into a chair, resting the back of her head against its rim. "This city is fabulous. Everything about it. Fabulous." She said she wanted to tell us a million things, but that she was almost too tired to do so. She handed each of us a pile of postcards that she had bought at various churches. "You'll love these," she said.

Edgar signaled the maitre d' from across the café, and we waited as he made his way to our table. "Red wine," Edgar said, pushing the menus away dismissively. "Any kind. As long as it's good."

My mother sighed, then began describing her day while I flipped through the stack of postcards. They were all of large, deeply colored paintings. In each, the baby Jesus seemed restless, the worshippers so awestruck they could barely stand.

A different waiter brought the wine and quickly poured it into three glasses, then left the bill on the table. Edgar pulled a credit card out of one of his pockets. "What about all of the money we changed at the airport?" my mother asked.

Edgar didn't have an answer.

"If you pay with a credit card, the conversion rate is better," I blurted, making it up. A moment slipped by in silence. We all held our glasses, but did not drink. "I read it in one of your books."

"Right," Edgar said. "That's true." He touched my glass with his. "Now we should have a toast. How about it?"

"Yes, a toast to us," my mother said, and we all clinked glasses. Then she and Edgar started making plans for dinner, mentioning places that had been suggested by their guidebooks, but for nothing after that. They were tired. They agreed that they were both exhausted. Sleep was what they needed.

Deep shadows were welling up from behind the columns of the arcade, and it was getting dark. My mother continued to talk about her tour. She spoke of gilded ceilings and the smell of incense, of intricate stone facades and the painted details of angels' wings. I stopped listening and wondered if someone had gone into my room and put sheets on my bed. Whether they had or not, I just hoped I would be able to sleep. Looking down into my glass, I saw that the long clouds in the sky were reflected as a shade of maroon in the wine. The sky itself was a deeper color. Even in the glass, the distinction was clear. Then, though it had gotten quiet and I could sense that my mother and Edgar were waiting for the answer to a question I hadn't heard, I swallowed almost all of my drink, feeling in my throat the sinking of the first stars of the night.

Round Trip

TECHNICALLY, CHRISTINE WAS off the clock, but she kept cruising around, hoping something would come up. She left the radio down low, that way she could keep tabs on Dawn, her niece, who was rummaging through the back of the truck. By the sound of it, the girl was breaking whatever she touched.

"I have to return this vehicle in the same condition I found it in," Christine said. "So quit poking around. You're making me nervous."

This was Christine's second week on the job. Driving an ice cream truck was the only work she could find, and it was easy enough, but it was suddenly starting to seem like the worst idea she'd ever had.

"I only wanted to see what was back there," Dawn said, closing one of the freezers, then the cool, sweet smell of the ice cream billowed into the air.

"Well, don't."

Dawn came and sat on the folding chair that was set up in place of a passenger seat. "You know, you're a pretty tense person," she said. "Maybe you should try taking deep breaths or something."

"Thanks for the suggestion."

Christine began searching for change in her pockets and along the dashboard, looking for enough to make a call. She needed to phone her sister and tell her where Dawn was, that she was all right. However, Christine hadn't spoken to her sister in six years. Calling her was simpler in principle than it would be in reality.

An hour ago, Christine had been doling out ice cream cones to a pack of kids in a park. Then Dawn had appeared at the serving window. She was a thin, dark, determined-looking girl, and Christine recognized her immediately; she was the spitting image of her mother. Dawn had a duffel bag in hand. She told Christine that she had just run away from home. The girl then announced that she wanted to live with Christine and climbed into the truck before Christine had an opportunity to say no. The notion that her mother would never agree to the request did not amount to much of an argument to her. Dawn was also pregnant, she said, and acted as if that did not pose a problem, either. Christine hadn't seen her niece since the last time she had seen her sister, but the news sent a pang of sadness through her. She felt for Dawn, though she had to admit that, for the time being, she was more concerned for herself. Christine couldn't help but worry about what was going to happen when her sister found out just who Dawn had run to.

"I like this weather," Dawn said. She rolled down her window and folded her arms over her stomach. She had not begun to show yet, and the denim cutoffs she was wearing fit her tightly.

"It's a little depressing, don't you think?" Christine asked.

A hard summer rainstorm had blown through town the previous night, and the roads were still a deep, wet black. Dislodged leaves covered the sidewalks and stuck to the truck's windshield. The sky was overcast, almost white, like a sheet the town had hidden itself under.

"Everything is a little depressing," Dawn said evenly, like that was an undeniable truth rather than a scrap of teenage philosophy.

Christine leaned into the steering wheel and looked up, as

though seeing the sky once more might change her mind. A day ago, the sun had been clear and blazing. The dull clouds now overhead only reminded Christine that her life, like the weather, was completely subject to change.

As they crossed the next intersection, Dawn sighed, "You're taking me home, aren't you?"

"I want to find a phone. To call your mother. I owe her that."

"I'm surprised you think you owe her anything." Dawn crossed her legs in a satisfied manner. "After all, the last time you saw her there was a different president in office."

In spite of the fact that they continued to live less than three miles from one another, the long silence between Christine and her sister seemed justified to her. Considering what had happened, her sister's behavior was entirely reasonable. Six years earlier, when Christine had been staying at her sister's place, a pot she'd left cooking on the stove caught fire and nearly burned the house down. Christine had been drunk and passed out on the couch at the time, with Dawn's younger brother asleep in a crib next to her. Christine only woke up after the fire trucks had arrived in front of the house. Now that she was living sober, Christine understood that what little trust her sister had left in her had gone up with the chairs and the curtains and the kitchen table.

When Christine found a gas station, she parked beside the pay phone. A few cars were lined up at the pumps. The sign listing the gas prices had been blown upside down by the storm. "Stay here," Christine ordered.

"What are you going to say to her?"

Good question, she thought, and left without answering.

Christine went into the phone booth and shut the door. From where she was, she could still see Dawn, which was the way she wanted to keep it until she could get the girl home. The pay phone's receiver was etched with initials, and curse words had been scratched into the coin box. Calling any one of the numbers that the graffiti suggested for a good time would have been easier than dialing her sister's number. It had been so long since Christine had heard her voice that she wondered if she would recognize it or, more importantly, if she would be able to speak once she did.

After the first ring, Christine glanced up to find that three children had gathered at the truck's now open serving window. Dawn was hanging her arm over the counter, pointing out suggestions. The ringing line was the only thing that kept Christine from bolting over there. It wasn't that she minded Dawn selling the ice cream—in truth, Christine needed the sales—but it made her self-conscious to see how quickly and easily her niece could slip into even that small part of her daily routine.

Nobody was answering at her sister's house. Christine expected an answering machine to come on any second, forcing her to decide whether or not to leave a message. Like a telegram from a foreign country, whatever she said would have to be precise and to the point. Christine wasn't ready for precision, so she hung up after hearing a few words of a voice she could not distinguish as her sister's or her niece's.

Christine threw open the booth's door more loudly than she had intended. The children all turned around and stared. "Don't mind her. She's a little stressed out," Dawn told them. Each one had a cone with a different scoop of ice cream on it.

"Are you trying to get me fired?" Christine demanded, storming toward the truck. "I'm sure you're breaking some sort of child labor law."

"Here," Dawn said, handing her the children's money through the serving window. "This way I can pay you back for the ride. Seeing as it's only one way," she said pointedly. "I think that should cover it, unless you charge more than the city bus."

Christine stuffed the change back into Dawn's hand. She wasn't mad, but it was easier to act like she was than to admit how comfortable she felt around Dawn, that she was even beginning to like her.

"What's the big deal anyway?" Dawn was leaning on the counter, peering down at Christine. "What was I supposed to do? A little boy knocked on the door."

"For starters," Christine said, "try staying out of sight. Your mother has probably called the police already. I don't want to get caught riding around with you when you're almost home."

"It's not like you abducted me."

Christine hoisted herself up into the driver's seat and started the truck. Dawn was right, but she still felt guilty, like simply being with her niece was as bad as what she had done six years ago.

"So what'd she say?" Dawn asked cautiously.

"Nothing," Christine answered. Dawn was visibly shocked, happy. "She wasn't home."

The girl's expression soured. She slipped the money into her pocket.

"We'll have to arrive unannounced, I guess," Christine said, heading out in the direction of her sister's place, "and knock on the front door."

She expected Dawn to put up a fight, to start squabbling or begging. Instead, her only remark was: "It's my house. I don't think I have to knock."

"No, it's the house you ran away from."

"I didn't run away," she shouted.

"You show up at the park. All you have is a duffel bag full of clothes. You don't have anyplace to go. And you tell me you're having a baby. That sounds like running away to me."

Dawn faced the window. "I didn't really run away. I ran to a specific person. You."

Back in the days when Christine was still speaking to her sister, Dawn had been a little girl, or at least in Christine's mind she was. She couldn't remember being close to her niece or even being around her that much, but because of her drinking, Christine's memory of those years was vague and unclear, like the almost transparent reflection of her face in the truck's slanted windshield. Christine had to wonder what her sister must have said that would make Dawn think she could turn to her. It could have been good or bad. Either might come off as appealing to a teenager.

"You really think she called the cops?"

"I don't know, but I'm not planning on going over the speed limit or anything. Just in case."

Dawn smirked.

"Don't laugh," Christine said. "We don't want to attract attention."

"Sure." Dawn gave her a look. "This truck is pretty hard to notice."

While they waited at a light, a breeze swept in through the windows, wafting up the sweet smell of the ice cream even stronger than before. It was a scent that Christine had acclimated to, but right then she could smell it just as she had when she first took the job, the dense sugary scent that tingled the nose.

"Where would you have gone if you couldn't find me today?" Christine asked seriously.

"Don't know."

Christine tried counting the yellow lines as they disappeared beneath the truck's hood; that way, she wasn't looking directly at her niece when she asked, "Are things at home bad? Is that why you left?"

Christine's sister had become a mystery to her, and the questions she thought of had the abstract quality of questions one might ask about a movie star: *What is it like to live with her? Is she different than I imagine her to be?* There was so much she would have liked to have known, but the snag in her conscience made her feel like she wasn't entitled to ask.

"Not terrible, I guess," Dawn said. "It's probably the same for me as it was for you."

Christine remembered sitting on her sister's front porch and listening to her scold the children for leaving toys strewn across the lawn, for running off the property, or for not wearing warmer coats. Eventually, she would turn her attention to Christine, how she could have been doing more with herself, how she didn't have her act together, how she drank too much. Her sister operated as though her own survival depended on how tight a reign she held on her family. For Christine, it had been the opposite. The less she knew about what went on, even in her own life, the easier everything became.

"I bet you don't miss living with her," Dawn said.

"That's different. Anyway, you said it wasn't terrible."

"But I left, didn't I?"

Christine pushed back her hair and slowed for a stop sign. "Things will work themselves out," she found herself saying, a generic piece of advice. She couldn't even come up with a cliché. "Your mother will be upset about you taking off the way you did, but she won't stay mad. She'll come around after awhile."

"She hasn't spoken to you in how long?"

"Sure, but . . ."

Christine let her voice trail off as she watched a flurry of propeller-shaped seedpods sift down out of a tree. She thought of her sister as a young girl, chasing them and trying to catch them before they hit the ground. She called it summer snow, and she said that any pod that touched the grass would melt. The point of the game was to save the pods, to catch them mid-air. At the time, Christine had little interest in rescuing seedpods, but she remembered admiring her sister for believing that she could save something, anything at all.

"She used to talk about you, you know," Dawn said softly, a tone that meant what her mother said was neither positive nor flattering.

"I don't blame her."

"Why not?"

"It was hard on her," Christine said. "I made things difficult."

"All I know is that I wouldn't want someone cutting me up behind my back. Least of all my own family."

Being separated from her sister was not as painful as it was strange. There were things that only she knew about Christine, events in their lives shared only by the two of them. Without her, Christine began to feel as though whole segments of her past weren't real, that the memories, now solely hers, were part of her imagination. When Dawn had showed up in the park, Christine instantly became aware of the blanks and how only her sister could fill them.

The road was leading into a wooded area. "Pull over," Dawn said.

"This isn't a taxi."

"Please pull over."

"What for?"

"I have to go to the bathroom."

"We're almost at your house. You can go there."

"No, I have to go bad. And you know what's going to happen when I get home. The second I walk in the door Mom's going to start in on me. I won't even make it to the living room."

Christine searched Dawn's face, unsure of her motives. "All right. But no funny stuff."

She parked on the shoulder and watched Dawn get out, ready to chase her if she ran. But the girl simply walked into the woods and squatted behind a tree.

"I guess I'm going to have to do this a lot from now on," Dawn yelled.

"You mean go to the bathroom outside?"

"No. Go to the bathroom period. I heard that when you're pregnant you have to go, like, every five minutes."

In the short time they had spent together, Christine had let herself forget that Dawn was truly pregnant. The idea hurt her now, more than she thought it could. Dawn hadn't mentioned anything about the father, and for that Christine was relieved. Not knowing made it easier to ignore the sharp reality of what was soon to be. From inside the truck, all Christine could see of her niece were her slim arms and legs and her bright sneakers contrasted against the fallen leaves. She looked like the girl Christine imagined she had once been, playing hide-and-seek. Only now, she was hiding, but it wasn't part of a child's game.

"So why didn't you ever have any kids?" Dawn shouted.

"My apartment's too small."

"Is it? I thought it would be big. It looks big from the outside." Dawn paused. "I found your address in the phone book. I hung around outside your building a couple of times sort of hoping you would look out your window and see me."

Hearing that made Christine's eyes burn. "I guess I don't look out my window enough."

Dawn stood up and moved away from the tree, buttoning her shorts and carefully tucking in her shirt. Surrounded by the bushes and shadows, she was completely out of place. Christine pictured her ending up right where she was, alone in the woods, then blocked out the image. Maybe they could work something out. She thought having Dawn around might be good for her. They could get along.

"Did you want to stay with me those times or were you just checking out the location?" Christine asked. She had to approach the subject slowly, gradually, instead of asking Dawn flat-out if she would really like to come and live with her. Christine wasn't even sure she could ask her directly.

"No, not really, I guess." Dawn, still concentrating on her shirt, missed the obvious disappointment on Christine's face. "I pretty much knew it couldn't happen."

"You're probably right. It would have gotten complicated," Christine replied, without really knowing what she meant.

"Anyway," Dawn said, hopping back up into the truck, "Mom would have hunted me down like a dog. She would've broken down your front door. And by the looks of it, you don't have the cash for a new one."

Christine couldn't help but laugh. "You've got that right."

No doubt, her sister was already trying to track Dawn down. If she found out that Dawn was staying with Christine, her sister would indeed kick in her door.

"One time when your mother lost one of your baby teeth, she tore the house apart looking for it. The place looked like a giant hand had picked it up and shook it."

Dawn nodded, listening but not remembering. "She can be like that."

A soft rattle in the engine reminded Christine that it was on, then she got back onto the road. Her sister was, if anything, predictable, and Christine figured that Dawn had grown up expecting clean sheets, well-balanced meals, and the strict attention of her mother—none of which Christine could offer her on a regular basis. The way she saw it, Dawn was better off with a sure thing rather than a maybe.

The speedometer hadn't crept over thirty-five, and Christine had been avoiding the main streets, opting for residential ones, which she hoped would get her to her sister's place without incident. But the next street she turned onto was blocked. The storm had downed a huge tree, and a crew of men was trying to cut it up to clear the road. There was one police officer on the scene, and when Christine caught sight of him, she cursed. He flagged her down, then made his way over to her window.

"Act normal," Dawn told her.

"Hi, ladies," the officer said, hands on hips. "What flavors do we have today?" He gave them a crooked smile, and they replied with a few light, staged laughs.

"I'll just back out of here," Christine said nervously, although driving the unwieldy truck in reverse was difficult to do.

"Don't bother. They're almost done. Won't be but a minute."

"But–"

Before she could try again, the officer had returned to the tree.

"See," Dawn said. "He didn't break out the handcuffs."

"Maybe he didn't get the APB."

Dawn sighed loudly.

"Fine," Christine said. "We'll wait."

The fallen tree was so tall that it spanned the width of the street, making it impassable. Two men with chainsaws were working simultaneously, slicing the trunk into massive rounds. Sawdust was flying off the blades like steam.

"I'm not scared," Dawn said, rubbing her hands over her knees. "Just so you know."

"About going home?"

"About the baby."

"Oh," Christine said. But she was sure that she was. She believed that Dawn was not only afraid of the baby, but of her future and the way it would unfurl in front of her. How could she not be?

The tree was now in pieces, some of which had already been rolled onto the sidewalk, making it look like some kind of unfinished puzzle. Fallen branches were scattered across the road. When the wind picked up, the leaves on the branches quivered. A gust of seedpods fluttered through the air, spinning past the men and the broken tree to the ground.

"It's like snow," Christine said.

"Sort of. Only it's green," Dawn teased.

Some of the seedpods bounced off the hood of the truck, and others got caught on the windshield wipers. Dawn took a purposeful breath. "Are you going to come in?" she asked.

"I don't know. I thought I'd decide later," Christine said, teasing her back.

"But we're almost there."

"Ask me in a minute," Christine said, putting her hands into her lap. "I'll make up my mind after they finish with the tree. Ask me after we drive around it."

Dawn didn't look at her. She focused her eyes straight ahead to wait. Christine wasn't sure what she was going to do, but she felt she soon would. Her stomach jumped with anticipation, then trembled in a way that she couldn't define as either fear or joy.

As the men cut into what was left of the trunk, small branches burst into the air like sparks. Beyond the tree, the road was light, no longer wet from the rain. Two of the men hauled the farthest wedge out of the road, then Christine put her hands back on the wheel. Before long, there would be room enough to pass.

In the City of the Living

IT WAS NEIL'S idea to take the last ferry out. All we had in front of us once we got to the mainland was eighteen hours on the highway, nothing that couldn't wait until the next day, but it was his car and he was driving.

A hard wind was coming off the water, and the late afternoon sun was shining dully on the half-dozen overpacked cars that filled the ferry's deck. Neil's older brother Wilson was in the backseat of the car pounding out a rhythm on the blanket that covered the torn upholstery. We thought he was drunk and that he might have taken something, too–some pills that he'd brought back with him from Raleigh–but we couldn't get him to tell us one way or the other. Whenever we asked, he'd just wag his finger at us and say, "That's just what's in the cards." Then he'd smile dreamily, as if his answer made perfect sense. Now, normally, Wilson was the type of guy who'd talk your ear off. Though in the half hour we'd spent together, he'd hardly said a word.

"This is going to be a problem," Neil whispered to me, motioning back at Wilson, who had fallen into the trance of his own impromptu percussion set.

"I'm neutral," I said. "I'm Switzerland. Leave me out of it."

For as long as I'd known them, Neil and Wilson had fought like the Hatfields and McCoys, so when I could, I tried not to get involved.

"Relax, man. No need to get all uptight," Neil said. "Come on, you should be stoked. You're finally getting off the island for good. I mean, hell, we both are. See ya later, suckers," Neil said with a laugh, then ceremoniously flipped off the stretch of land that was drifting into the distance behind the ferry.

It wasn't that I didn't share Neil's excitement. I *was* happy to be getting away from home, but my version of good-bye didn't involve the middle finger. It was August, and we were on our way to Memphis, where I'd gotten a scholarship at a small college. Neil was making the drive as a favor to me. In return, he was going to stay on, living in my dorm room until he could find a job and an apartment of his own. That was as much of a plan as he had. And to him it seemed like more than enough.

Earlier that afternoon, my father had stood at my bedroom door and watched as I packed the last of my clothes. "It'll be good for you to be somewhere different for a change," he'd said. He was leaning against the doorjamb, trying to look casual. We'd silently agreed to keep any discussion of my leaving to a minimum. He held the doorknob and gently turned it back and forth, saying, "You were probably sick of this place anyway." We both knew he was right.

"You couldn't pay me to go back," Neil said, then he gave a loud whoop out the window and thrust his fist into the air triumphantly, turning the heads of the tourists who were on their way home from their summer vacations on the Outer Banks. Given half the opportunity, Neil would have gotten up onto the bridge and pushed the ferry to full throttle to get us to the mainland more quickly. That was his personality; he only operated in extremes, which made him exciting to be around, but he could also be a real pain in the ass. Life couldn't come at Neil fast enough and, in that way, I guess I admired him.

"We're going to Memphis, boys," Wilson announced, popping his head up between the front seats and startling Neil and me on purpose. "Birthplace of the King," he said in a bad Elvis accent, then fell back into his seat and giggled in a dim, stoned way. I was pretty sure that Elvis hadn't been born in Memphis, but I didn't feel like starting anything with Wilson. He was only supposed to be coming along for part of the trip. We were going to drop him off at a bar near the dock where, he claimed, he was meeting up with some guys who needed a drummer for their band. With Wilson, it was often difficult to tell what was true and what he'd made up just to make himself look good.

"Elvis is buried in Memphis, too, right?" he asked.

"I guess," Neil said, pushing his long, straggly hair behind his ear. He was starting to go bald on top and, if it wasn't for the length of his hair, you could mistake him for Wilson from behind, a fact Neil was intensely aware of.

"Well, if it's good enough for the King, then it's good enough for Domino." Wilson held up a small cardboard box, then shook it. Inside the box were the ashes of his ex-girlfriend's dog. There were problems between them, but the dead dog was the least of them. Wilson had stolen the box from the girl after she had broken up with him, and he'd kept it close ever since.

"Man, throw that stuff overboard," Neil told him. "A burial at sea. That's good enough. Tell him, Doug."

Thankfully, I didn't get the chance to answer.

"No way," Wilson protested with bleary-eyed indignance. "This dog is not going out like that. Just dust in the wind and all. The seagulls will eat him. Or the fish. That would be a total disruption of nature's food chain."

Typical logic for Wilson, drunk or not, and there was no use attempting a rebuttal.

Outside on the deck, people were lining up along the railings to watch the island we had called home fade into the summer haze. Most appeared sad, some even wistful, as if they might take out a handkerchief like in old movies and wave, as though the island were a lover disappearing into the horizon for good. I'd lived there all my life, and I knew that when the season was over the island didn't simply drop off the map.

In the side mirror I could see Wilson staring at the little box and stroking it gingerly like he couldn't bear to part with it.

"This dog," he declared, "this dog deserves to go out in style."

With little to do on the hour-long ferry ride, we simply sat in the car listening to the radio. It was that time of day when you could feel the invisible pressure of the sun through the clouds even though the sky was the same color as the sea foam in the ferry's wake — a flat, unimpressive white. Children were laughing and running between the cars parked on deck, their bare feet slapping against the metal sheeting. Bored, I waved to one of the kids. The little girl, whose tight, pointy braids stuck out at odd angles from her head, simply stood there waving back, and she wouldn't stop. When Wilson spotted her, he pretended to strangle himself, bugging out his eyes and gripping his neck until the girl ran away, virtually in tears. Wilson found the whole thing amusing. I acted like I hadn't seen him. Neil rolled his eyes.

"Hey, can't we get out of the car," Wilson whined. "I'm dying in here. I need something to drink or I'm going to pass out. For real."

Such exaggerations were standard issue Wilson. That was part of the reason Neil was so anxious to get away. Wilson had moved to Raleigh earlier that year to start a band, only to return months later flat broke from partying like the rock star he hadn't become. Neil resented his brother for leaving, but he resented him even more for coming home, for wasting his chance. Granted, Wilson wasn't the most well-adjusted person, but he wasn't a bad guy. He was short and thin and relatively unremarkable, so he talked big to get attention. The only problem was that if nobody cut him off, Wilson could go on for hours, literally nonstop, driving Neil to a point where I could watch his jaw grind. Once, Neil had slammed his brother's hand in a door just to make him shut up. All our lives I'd been the one playing referee in their sparring matches, but lately there had been times when I was afraid to get between them. Neil was at the end of his rope when it came to Wilson, and I wasn't sure how much more he could take before he really snapped.

I had convinced Neil to come with me to Memphis for a few days without knowing what it would lead to. For years we'd talked about moving to the mainland and fantasized about being able to go to the movies whenever we wanted, about being able to buy our clothes from a store instead of a mail-order catalog, even about getting good reception on the television. We couldn't wait. After Neil had decided to move, we didn't discuss it much, though we both knew that, whether he found a job in Memphis or not, the odds were he wouldn't be coming back, that he might never cross this stretch of water to the island again.

"You guys want to get some taffy at the snack bar?" Wilson asked. He sounded spacey. He dug in his pockets for money and only came up with change.

"The taffy at the snack bar is turn-of-the-century. You shouldn't eat it," I said. "It never sells, and they never throw it away. You could crack a tooth." I didn't know this for sure, but for as many times as I'd ridden the ferry with nothing to do but mill around memorizing the names that were carved into the wooden observation benches, I felt I would've noticed a change as small as a new box of taffy in the display case.

Wilson was oblivious to my remarks. He hopped out of the car. "Are you two coming or what?"

Neil was tuning him out, so I said, "We're right behind you."

Wilson shrugged and padded off. Once he was out of earshot, Neil said, "I think he's faking it."

"Faking it? You mean he's not really high?"

"Doubtful. And there were only two cans of beer in the cooler. So he's not drunk, either."

The car seat had grown hot, and I could feel the backs of my legs sticking to it. I moved, and my skin made a ripping sound as it pulled away from the upholstery.

"Why would Wilson try to pull one over on us?" I asked.

"Don't you get it? It's so we don't ditch him. If he thinks I'm staying in Memphis, he'll want to stay too."

Neil could get a little nuts when it came to Wilson; he suspected him of everything from lying and petty thievery (which he was actually guilty of on a regular basis) to elaborate, well-organized schemes. Between Neil's paranoia and the heat, I was beginning to think I should have gone for taffy with Wilson.

"I think you're giving him too much credit," I said.

"Oh, no. Wilson might play dumb, but he's not too dumb to pass up a good thing."

Maybe, I thought. Island life left us with few prospects job-wise. You were either a fisherman or a tradesman or you owned some sort of shop that made you solely dependent on the summer traffic for your yearly income. Each job was about as steady as a boat on a windy day. It wasn't much of an option. My folks had a grocery store and, besides the boat repair shop, theirs was one of the only stable businesses in town. Fortunately, they didn't begrudge me for wanting to leave. "You can do whatever you want, son," my father would say. "But there's a lot you can't do if you stay here."

If Neil was right and Wilson was acting, it was only to avoid what we all saw as an inevitable dead end. Wilson had nodded off a few times, then woken up rambling. His eyes wouldn't stay focused and he couldn't keep his hands still. If it was a show, it was a good one. If it wasn't, then he was truly in rough shape. Either way, I kind of felt bad for the guy.

"Well," I said. "What do we do with him?"

"I don't know, man. Let's get him near the railings. Maybe he'll fall overboard."

We locked up the car, though there wasn't much worth stealing inside, and headed to the back of the ferry where we could get down to the lower deck. Neil paused at the top of the stairs as if a lightbulb had gone on in his head, and I almost ran into him.

"What?" I asked.

"I was just thinking. There's this rest stop off the highway," he said. "It's got a little park and phones and vending machines. A lot of people use the bathrooms there and stuff."

"Yeah, so?"

"What if we asked Wilson to get us some candy, then took off?" Neil said.

We were standing in the cool, shadowy corridor, and I could feel my sweaty clothes hanging off of me, weighing on my skin. Neil wasn't talking about a prank; we wouldn't be going back for Wilson. I guess I hadn't thought that Wilson was serious about coming all the way to Memphis with us, but the way Neil looked at me, waiting for me to agree, to back him up, convinced me just how serious he was about leaving his brother behind.

"It wouldn't be a big deal," Neil said, trying to sell me on the idea. "We're not even that far from home. Or hey, he could call those guys he's supposed to be meeting up with. That is, if they exist." Neil saw that I wasn't biting, so he changed his tactic. "Hell, Doug, it's like we're those guys in *Escape from Alcatraz*. Get out at all costs."

"Don't you think you're being a little melodramatic?"

"Wilson's deadweight. We need to get rid of him before he drags us down with him."

This was the height of irrationality, even for Neil. I couldn't help but picture rats crawling over one another while fleeing a sinking ship. As it happened, the ocean was getting a little choppy, and the ferry weighed in every roll with a heady buck. The noise from the engine was loud in the hallway. It seemed to be coming from every direction.

Neil had always been good at rallying the troops, at getting me on his side. Usually, it worked. But this was different. We weren't trying to escape from Alcatraz. We were just a couple of guys who'd dreamed of cutting out new lives for ourselves in a city that was still a tiny name on a map. More importantly, Neil didn't seem to remember that only one of the guys in the movie lived. Or maybe he did. I had to wonder which guy he thought I was.

When we got below deck, we found Wilson sitting alone on a bench, zoned-out with the box of ashes cradled in his arms. "What's the good word, brothers? Couldn't resist the call of the taffy, could ya?"

"Where's yours?" I asked.

"I got sidetracked, if you know what I mean," he said, nodding toward the girl behind the counter at the snack bar. She wore feather earrings, a tank top, and the distinct expression of someone who had better things to do.

"She saw something she liked," Wilson said with a wink.

"Are you trying to say that that girl was putting the moves on you?" I asked.

There was a short line of people at the snack bar, and the girl was serving up sodas and bags of chips with the same apathetic look.

"What about Tracy?" Neil asked dryly.

"What about her?" Wilson was either disregarding the dig at his failed relationship, or he was too out of it for the wisecrack to sink in.

Neil had let me in on some of the more private details of Wilson's affairs, and I knew that Tracy, Wilson's ex, had been pregnant, but that she had miscarried in a toilet at a sandwich shop. The next day, her dog was hit by a car. Her run of bad luck then turned into Wilson's. She told him that it was all too much for her to handle and that, as a boyfriend, he was bringing her down. When he asked her why they couldn't stay together, she'd said, "That's just what's in the cards." The same thing he'd been telling us all day.

"So should I talk to her or what?" Wilson asked eagerly.

"She's not even looking at you," I said.

"What's that supposed to mean?" His mouth hung open and he looked honestly confused.

"Nothing. Forget I said it."

"Poor girl. She doesn't know what she's in for," Wilson said, then he gave my shoulder a slap and sauntered over to the snack bar.

I turned to Neil. "You know he's, like, out of his skull, right?"

"You shouldn't encourage him."

"I didn't encourage him. I was just answering him."

"Same difference," Neil said.

He walked over to the opposite wall where vintage maps of North Carolina hung, all tattered and yellowed with age the way one would imagine a treasure map to be. Neil was ignoring me on purpose, trying to guilt me into agreeing to dump Wilson off at the rest stop. Neil had been my best friend, and part of me wanted to take his side purely out of allegiance. Still, I couldn't. Sure, Wilson would get home somehow, but it was the principle of the matter. I kept waiting to hear Neil say he was kidding, that he was just pulling my leg, but he wasn't talking.

I went over and stood next to him, my form of a truce. He leaned over to one of the maps titled "The Outer Banks: A Coastal Oasis," and started to trace our route to Memphis with his finger.

"It won't take us that long to get there," Neil said. "It could be worse." He was trying to sound nonchalant, like it wouldn't be any skin off his back if Memphis were a bust. But it was obvious how much he wanted everything to work out.

"Do you know what Memphis means?" my father had asked as I closed my suitcase that morning. I wasn't sure if he was trying to be philosophical, if it was a rhetorical question or the opening to a parting speech that he had prepared, but I stopped what I was doing and waited for him to finish. "Literally, it means 'The City of the Living' in Egyptian. Or it used to. I read that somewhere. Thought you should know. Just in case somebody asks you when you get there."

Watching Neil study the huge map, it dawned on me that he was as much of a sinking ship as Wilson, and he knew it. Now they were both holding on to Memphis, to me, for dear life.

"This map is old," Neil said.

"Yeah. I can't believe our island's even on it."

Neil finally faced me. "Maybe it shouldn't be."

A loud thud came from across the room. Neil and I turned around and saw Wilson splayed across the ground in front of the snack bar. The girl with the feather earrings folded her arms in a huff.

"That creep tried to touch me," she said to one of the on-lookers. "I mean, gross. I'm, like, working."

Wilson's shirt and shorts were soaked. An empty cup lay on the counter. The floor beneath him was wet, which meant that he'd probably slipped after the girl had thrown the drink at him. Everyone in the room was gawking.

Neil could hardly look at his brother. He stormed off onto the top deck. I tried to help Wilson up from the floor, but he shooed me away as if I were cramping his style, then straightened his shirt and strutted toward the stairs in an attempt to look unfazed. The cardboard box of ashes lay in a puddle of soda. Wilson must have dropped it when he fell.

"Sorry," I said to no one in particular, then picked up the box and headed after him.

On deck, a couple was posing for pictures. The light had changed, and they were using the dusky, pink outline of the coast as their backdrop. Neil was over by the railings, chewing the inside of his cheek in annoyance. Wilson sprawled out onto an observation bench and kicked up his feet as if nothing had happened.

"Can you believe that?" he asked in sincere disbelief. "One minute the girl wants me. The next, it's like *bam*. What a tease." He looked at his stained shorts. "Now I've got to let this dry or people are going to stare."

Neil shot me a look that meant people would stare anyway.

"Memphis," Wilson said, testing the sound of the word. "There's got to be plenty of babes in a city like that." He put his hands behind his head. "They're going to be lining up when I get there. Hell, they'll have to take numbers. I'll have to get one of those electronic Now Serving signs."

Neil gripped the metal railing in a stranglehold. His back seemed to tick off each of Wilson's remarks with tiny spasms. The wind was sharp, rippling his shirt, but Neil was too tense to move. It was like watching somebody shake a bottle, watching the bubbles build toward the top. I held my breath, bracing myself.

"Yeah," Wilson said, "I think Memphis will be good to me."

That was it. Neil whipped around. "What are you talking about? You couldn't even keep the girlfriend you had. And when she finally broke up with you, you stole her dead dog. That's pitiful. You're pitiful." Neil's face tightened in disgust. "It probably wasn't even your baby anyway."

In that moment, the wind seemed to stop and the boat ceased to rock. Before I knew it, Wilson had jumped up and pinned Neil to the railing, bending him backwards toward the water. Neil was landing punches on Wilson's chest and stomach while Wilson held his throat. Now the world came back in a fury. The air was hissing, and the boat lurched. Every swell of the ocean beneath the ferry seemed to coincide with the moves of the fight.

I tried to get in between them, but Wilson had a stronghold on Neil's neck, and he was choking him hard. Neil went for his eyes with his thumbs, but Wilson wouldn't let go. I finally got my elbow into Wilson's ribs and was able to shove them apart.

Neil cursed and spat a couple of times. Wilson was walking around in a circle, breathing hard and holding his side. Fortunately, no one had seen the fight.

"See," Neil said to me, rubbing his neck. He was acting angry, provoked, justified. But it was suddenly, painfully clear to me that it was exactly that, an act, just like the one he'd claimed Wilson was performing for us. Neil had said the thing about the baby on purpose. "See," he said.

Neil took the car keys out of his pocket and started toward the other end of the ferry where we'd parked. Wilson and I had no choice but to follow him.

When he unlocked the car and we opened the doors, each of us was met with a gust of hot, trapped air. It was a relief from the wind and what had just happened. No one spoke, yet there was a certain clarity to the moment, like when an overfilled balloon finally pops. Neil wanted me to want Wilson gone as bad as he did, so he had baited Wilson, hoping the fight would make me think better of the rest stop idea. Neil had decided that if Wilson was going to get off the island, he wasn't going to do it on his coattails. My friend was too caught up to catch the irony in that.

I cranked down my window and a humid dusk breeze rushed over my face. The dock was in view. People had begun climbing into their cars. The summer was over, but the night would be warm. It wouldn't feel like the end of anything.

After the ferry docked, a horn sounded, signaling that it was safe for drivers to pull off the deck. Cars were slowly rolling onto solid land. Neil started the engine. He turned on the radio and kept his eyes nailed to the road in front of us. Wilson took out the one map we'd brought for the trip and spread it out over his knees. I thought about the map I'd seen on the ferry that said the Outer Banks was an oasis on the coast. I reminded myself that to believe that any place was an oasis, you had to think you were in a desert to begin with. Memphis had become a sort of shimmering promise in all of our minds and, as we drove, it seemed as though it lay somewhere out there beyond the sand dunes.

"I'm sort of hungry," Neil said. He was riding the brake, lining up behind the other cars to get onto the highway.

"I guess I could eat," Wilson said, tough, his ego still bruised.

"I'm fine," I said. "I can wait."

I felt Neil glance at me. If he was going to go through with it, I wasn't going to help him. I wanted to hear him say it.

"No. We should stop," Wilson went on. "We need to buy some extra food anyway. It's a pretty long drive."

The on-ramp was coming up. I pulled the box of ashes from my pocket, where I had forgotten about it, though it had been pressing its outline into my leg. I passed it back to Wilson.

"Thanks, man," he said. He took the box from my hands with care. "This dog is going to be laid to rest properly in Memphis. I'm going to make sure of that."

Outside, the dune grass was swaying from the wind coming off the road, ushering us on. The paper flyers for summer corn and boat rentals that were staked in the sand fluttered and shook with each passing car. A sign for the interstate exit and the rest stop stood up ahead. Surrounded by all of that movement, it was a still point in the world until we passed it. The radio was on low, but it seemed like if we drove fast enough it would get louder, that we'd get closer to the sound. Then we could hear whatever we wanted to hear.

On a Clear Day

DEIRDRE WAS ALMOST home when she remembered what her husband had asked her. She'd spent most of the afternoon trying, unsuccessfully, to think of what he'd said, then the memory came to her so suddenly that she nearly ran a red light.

It was simple. He wanted a bottle of wine to have with dinner, one that was foreign and extravagant. They deserved something nice for a change, he had said that morning, passing her some extra money. "We have it coming."

There was an upscale liquor store on her way home that carried all of the best wines, and as Deirdre pulled into the parking lot, it occurred to her that the store was halfway from her house and Peter's apartment, where she had just come from. It was practically right in between the two, something she wished she hadn't noticed.

A bell above the door jingled when she entered the store. The man behind the counter, heavy and hunched on his stool, was talking on the telephone. He nodded a hello. "Go on, finish your story," he said into the receiver, then walked into the back-room behind the counter, pulling the phone cord along with him.

Deirdre wound her way through the aisles to the rear of the store. It had once been a used book shop, and the wood paneling and brass fixtures remained, giving the place the feel of a library. Deirdre didn't know much about selecting the right color wine or a good year; the subject had never really interested her. She'd planned on asking for help, but the man seemed to be deep in conversation and she didn't have the energy to interrupt.

Peter had made a point of ordering a specific Chardonnay the first time the two of them had had dinner together, one that turned out to be too dry for Deirdre's taste, though she didn't say so. In the end, Peter spilled his glass onto the table while laughing at something she'd said that was only mildly funny. He was the type of person who tried too hard at everything, so hard it made her tired of him. Deirdre didn't remember what it was that had attracted her to him in the first place, and she wasn't sure why she bothered to see him for as long as she did. Like the topic of wine, all she knew was that she didn't care deeply enough to commit any of the details to memory. Peter was not what she wanted or what she was looking for. What that was, she still couldn't say.

Deirdre heard the man from the counter laughing on the phone. "Now come on," he demanded in jest. "That can't be true."

She picked up a bottle with an attractive label and held it, then the bell over the door rang, and she put the bottle back, unsure. Nothing was jumping out at her. She leaned against the shelf at the end of the aisle and crossed her arms, resisting the urge to slide down and sit on the floor.

Earlier that day, Deirdre had made a decision: she was going to stop seeing Peter. She'd also made up her mind to confess the affair to her husband. There had been others, but he never knew. They were unmemorable men who had drifted by like months on the calendar. Deirdre had slipped on the smooth surface of her life–she didn't know how many times–but had never felt herself fall. She'd been in midair for so long that she yearned to hit the ground, if only to be sure it was there.

"Wait. I have to stand up," the man from the counter declared in disbelief. "I can't take this story sitting down."

Deirdre had met her husband six years earlier at a dentist's office. "I have a cavity," he had said, pacing the waiting room. "I've never had one before. I've never been drilled."

Once they began dating, Deirdre realized that his dental record seemed to reflect his entire character, unspoiled and intact, and she was drawn to what she saw as a promising wholeness. He was a serious, well-meaning man who was deep into his forties, some years older than Deirdre, and had never been married. To him, her restless spirit was charming, a sign of heart, her past divorce not a black mark on her life but simply a bad match. In his eyes, she could do no wrong. He'd given her too much credit, she thought, far more than she had ever given herself, and that was what she felt the worst about.

"Could you shut up? Could you be quiet for one goddamn second?" This was a different voice Deirdre heard. It was closer, a sharp whisper.

Another voice answered, "I'm only saying we could have waited. It's the friggin' middle of the afternoon."

"Keep pissing me off and you're walking home. It's my motorcycle."

"It's your brother's, asshole."

There was a dull thud. Deirdre guessed that one of them had pushed the other. To her, they sounded like high-school kids, teenagers with pimples and dirty fingernails.

"Whatever," the first one said. "Save the gangster act for the guy at the register."

Deirdre's breath came fast and hard. She couldn't believe what was happening, but she felt no fear, only shock coiling around her body like a rope. Her thoughts came in rapid fire, like someone flicking channels on a television. She pictured herself in her car, in the store's parking lot, coming through the door. She remembered sitting on Peter's sofa an hour earlier, willing herself to recall what her husband had wanted. Peter was asking her what she was thinking about and she said, "Nothing." Then he pressed his lips into her hair and she felt his teeth beneath them.

"Come on," one of the guys whispered.

"Why do we have to do it now? This place is open late. Let's come back when it's dark out."

"Chickenshit."

Deirdre thought she heard a bag being unzipped, but she didn't dare turn the corner to check. The reality of the situation hung over her like an open umbrella. She felt its presence, but little cover or protection. She imagined what other people might think or do at a moment like this: scream for help, bolt for the back door, pray to God. She could not yell or run; she couldn't bring herself to those reactions. And she did not believe in God, only the random, wrong, unavoidable way the world worked. She was part of the world too, she thought.

"Why can't we do it tomorrow?" the younger one pleaded.

The other cursed under his breath in frustration. Deirdre took her chance and moved silently down the aisle, head low, hoping they would not see her between the spaces in the shelves.

When she got to the front, the man behind the counter was hanging up the telephone. "Oh," he said. "I thought I heard you leave. Boy, could I tell you a whopper of a story," he sighed, chuckling to himself.

Deirdre was trying to listen over the man's voice as he spoke to see if she could sense where the two guys were.

"What can I help you with?" the man asked cheerily.

She mouthed the word *robbery* slowly, drawing it out.

"Pardon me?" he asked, confused.

She did it again.

"I'm sorry, ma'am. I can't hear you."

A board creaked in the back of the store. Deirdre searched

the man's face, hoping he had noticed. He hadn't. He was still waiting for her to answer.

"Are you looking for something in particular?"

Desperation flooded her. She glanced around at the counter, the register, the lottery machine, even the donation can for lost children, racking her brain for a way to convey what she knew. Nothing came to her. There was a glass case behind the counter. In it sat a dusty bottle, the label cracked with age. It was the first thing Deirdre could focus on, and she pointed to it on impulse. "That," she said. "I want that."

"Oh lady, do you even know what that is? It's a Saint Emilion 1959." He paused. "It's a three-hundred dollar bottle of wine."

"It's for my husband." That was all Deirdre could manage to say.

She thought of the time right after they were married when she had spent half her savings to buy him a watch he'd mentioned in passing, of the days when she'd made him lie in bed with her for hours on end. She had buffeted him with an impatient, fitful kind of love, as though putting down payments on a debt she knew she would incur. She hated knowing herself so well.

"Wow. He's a lucky guy," the man said. He took the bottle from the case, holding it delicately. His fingers left marks in the dust. "Too bad you aren't going to have a pretty night to enjoy it. It's supposed to rain. Should be beautiful tomorrow, though," he added. "Knock on wood."

While the man rang up the wine, Deirdre saw an opportunity. She frantically dug out her credit card to pay him, and when he gave her the slip to sign, she scribbled him a note explaining what was about to happen.

"Yeah, my nephew's coming over tomorrow with his model airplane," the man said, making conversation. "We're going to fly it in the park." He took a paper bag from beneath the register and shook it open. "I'm just crossing my fingers that it's sunny.

You know, a clear day at least. A model airplane on a clear day is something to see."

Deirdre pictured the plane against the sky and her heart shuddered.

"It's like that movie *On a Clear Day You Can See Forever*," the man said. He slipped the bottle of wine into a bag and folded the top neatly. "Barbra Streisand's in it. Ever see it?"

Deirdre felt like she was watching a china plate that was balanced precariously on top of a pole. Then it hit her: that was the way she'd felt for a long time. She could not imagine what her husband would do when he found out about her affair but that, she realized, was the whole point.

"No," she answered, suddenly aware that the two guys must have been listening, waiting. "I haven't seen that one."

Deirdre slid her credit card receipt across the counter purposefully, face-up so the man could read it, and kept her thumb on the paper's edge.

"You should rent it," the man told her. Then he snagged the slip out from under her finger and stuffed it into a drawer without a glance.

He handed her the bottle of wine. "Your husband better appreciate this," he said, flashing her a smile.

Deirdre's mind sputtered and swam until it locked on the sad, single fact that the man had no idea what awaited him. She watched him pick up a newspaper, then found herself stepping away from the counter and walking, automatically, toward the door. Before she opened it, she turned back. The two guys were nowhere in sight. For a second she allowed herself to believe that she had dreamed them, that their whispers were only in her head. She watched the man smooth the paper out in front of him and reminded herself that the voices were undeniably, regrettably real. Deirdre opened the door, sounding the bell, and the man looked up.

"Have a nice night," he said. "Drive safely."

Future Tense

I WAS IN THE bathroom at a bus station washing my hands when the guy next to me started to cry. It was a frigid evening in the dead of winter, 1978, and he and I were the only people in there. The guy was dirty and dressed in layers of ill-fitting clothes, clearly homeless, but he didn't look quite as shabby or run-down as the other men I'd seen sleeping on the snow-covered steam grates outside the station. He took a rag from his pocket and wiped his face with it. He was a young man, probably not over thirty, maybe even my age at the time–twenty-five.

I dried my hands, acting as if I didn't see him. But the guy was staring at me while he wept, trying to force me to acknowledge him. I couldn't remember ever having seen a man cry like that, such unabashed, earnest tears. The honest truth was that I was almost afraid to meet his gaze. When I finally did, he whimpered, "My friend's outside, and he's dying."

He waited for my response. I didn't have one. But not because I was shocked by what he'd said. As far as I could tell, that was the sort of thing that happened in bus stations at night. A buddy and I were traveling down from Boston to Baltimore for the holidays, me to see my parents, him for his wife and son. On account of a snowstorm we'd missed our connection in Newark, stranding us and another dozen or so people until the next bus could arrive. By the time we got there, my buddy and I had already seen one woman vomit, two men fist-fighting over a candy bar from the vending machine, and handful of drunken bums stumbling through the station singing a chorus of "Oh Holy Night."

"And I thought Moscow bus stations were bad," my friend, Yuri, had said.

Yuri was Russian, and he didn't speak much English, which meant he didn't speak much at all. Back then, that was exactly the kind of friend I needed. I'd met him at the heating and air-conditioning repair school I'd just dropped out of. The classes were short and easy enough, but a box of cheap tools upon graduation didn't seem worth the effort. Those days, nothing did.

Something inside of me, right beneath the skin, had gone numb without reason or justification. Everything that had interested and concerned me ceased to be important. It was as if my brain had been pumped full of air, causing the world to go mute, then life was reduced to a matter of going through the motions. So having some homeless guy tell me that a man outside was dying had about as much effect on me as the water I'd toweled off my hands did.

"You look like a doctor," the guy said hopefully. "I bet you could help him."

The fact that this guy thought I looked like a doctor told me a lot about the sort of person I was dealing with. The reflection that met me in the mirror over the sink was haggard and grungy, in dire need of a shower, a shave, a bed. I looked as grim as I felt. I'd been on a bus for the past six hours, sweating in my heavy clothes, which weren't even clean to begin with. Even so, I liked the idea that I could be mistaken for a doctor.

"A water heater is about the only thing I'd be able to fix," I confessed.

"Good enough," the guy said with the nervous optimism

of someone who was either truly scared or truly crazy. He told me his name was Ben, then he broke for the door, expecting me to follow him.

And to my surprise, I did.

Yuri was sitting on a bench waiting for me, feet resting atop his suitcase. He had his cassette player out, and he was listening to these "Teach Yourself English" tapes with an earpiece. We'd barely spoken on the ride down from Boston, but I'd heard him whispering his lessons, his thick accent turning the phrases into a kind of chant: "I went to the store. I am going to the store. I am going to go to the store."

When he saw me rush by, Yuri called out, his English choppy but distinct, "James, where are you going?"

Most of the other passengers had fallen asleep sprawled out on the rows of benches and, like Yuri, none had noticed Ben, who was now sprinting toward the other side of the station.

"Come on," I shouted to Yuri and kept going. I wasn't sure what had gotten into me. Chasing after Ben had been more a reflex than a conscious decision.

Yuri must have thought I was running to get another bus because when he caught up to me he was carrying both of our bags, the weight of which would have toppled me after a few steps. He was a small but sturdy man in his forties with the hard hands of a farmer, the life he had left behind for a better one, fixing refrigerators in America. Yuri had been forced to leave his wife and their young son in Baltimore with relatives in order to move to Boston. A cousin of his had offered to let him, but only him, live there rent-free and to help pay for him to learn a trade. It was an opportunity he couldn't pass up.

Yuri kept a miniature calendar in his wallet so he could keep track of how long it would be until he could see his family again. "I am thinking of tomorrow, not of this day," he would declare after class, crossing out each date. "I am keeping my head there so this day will go more fast. But sometimes I am worrying tomorrow will not be better. That tomorrow is other word for not so soon."

I lead Yuri toward the corridor I'd seen Ben turn down, and we found ourselves in a deserted hallway. The bright, fluorescent lights and the smell of cleaning fluid made it feel as if we were jogging through an empty swimming pool. The sound of our shoes hitting the floor ricocheted off the tiled walls.

"Why we are running, James?" Yuri asked, panting.

"If I tell you, you'll stop," I said, then I spotted Ben huddled in a corner near the back entrance to the station, and somebody was lying on the ground next to him.

"Hurry up," Ben hollered. "I think it's too late."

I wasn't prepared for what I saw next. Slumped on the floor beside Ben was a man in his late fifties, blood drying in his silvery beard, one side of his face beaten black. One of his eyes was swollen shut, and from the way he was holding his arm, it must have been broken, maybe some ribs too. His leg was propped up on his bloodstained jacket, no doubt damaged as well. Yuri froze mid-stride when he realized what he was looking at.

"It's going to be okay, Marvin," Ben said, comforting the man. "I found somebody who can fix things."

Yuri slowly set his suitcase on the floor. "James, please to be telling me what is going on?"

The sheer sight of this battered man overwhelmed me. I was too shaken to answer. However, Marvin lifted his head when he heard Yuri's voice. He opened his good eye and squinted at him.

"Butch?" Marvin called dreamily. "Butch, is that you?" He tried to smile, but his lips pinched into a wince.

"Sorry," Ben said. "Marvin can get a little confused. He has this thing about *Butch Cassidy and the Sundance Kid*."

Marvin groaned, and Ben pulled a bottle of Coke from his pocket to give him a drink. This was some scene, I thought. Me, some flaky kid, a delirious old man who'd been beaten to a pulp, and a Russian immigrant who probably thought we were all nuts. It seemed like the opening to a bad joke, and I was in it.

Marvin started sputtering on the soda and choking. "So you can help him, right?" Ben asked, looking to Yuri, then to me.

Yuri bent down and inspected Marvin's wounds, then his

face grew grave. "We need to be calling police or hospital or . . . what is word?"

"An ambulance? No way." Ben shook his head vehemently. "Marvin won't let those emergency people near him. He's afraid of 'em. Said he saw them electrocute somebody once."

"Electrocute?" Yuri didn't understand. "But his leg, I can tell it is broke."

Ben stood his ground. Yuri turned to me, bewildered.

Marvin was a mess and what he needed was a doctor, a real one, pronto. But since Ben wouldn't let us get any help, there was little more I could do other than to ask, "What happened to him?"

"These two jerks who deal around here," Ben explained. "They're always cruising up and down this street. But they're not big time. They're just bullies with a car. All Marvin did was spit in their direction."

"They kicked me when I was down, Butch," Marvin wheezed. "They fought dirty. I needed you, Butch. Where were you?" His question was cut short by a fit of coughing. When he caught his breath, he went on. "I woke up outside in the snow. I couldn't feel a thing. Not my fingers or my toes. I licked my lips and they felt like cold rubber."

This description was apparently for my benefit. Marvin probably thought he was helping me with my diagnosis. From what he'd said, all I could tell him was that I sympathized. I knew exactly how he felt. I'd been walking around for the past few weeks without feeling my legs move or my feet touch the ground.

I had stopped going to school, let all of my bills go, and was about to be evicted. *Why bother*, I thought. I could no longer see anything on the horizon. The future wasn't bleak, it was blank. Returning home to my parents, to their inevitable disappointment and disapproval, only promised to make matters worse. But I had no other choice. I'd been bounced out of every college in the greater Boston area for screwing around and skipping class, and my parents had cut me off. They were fed up with second chances. For them, this would be the last straw. Worse yet, I wouldn't be able to explain my behavior to them. I couldn't even explain it to myself. All I knew was that somewhere, somehow, a switch had been flipped, one that I wouldn't simply be able to talk myself into flicking back to normal.

"I just wanted to die with my boots on," Marvin announced, then resumed coughing.

Yuri pulled me aside. "Back at my village, I have seen men like this, hurt in accidents with tractor or kicked by mule. This man, Marvin, he has boot print on side of his head. We cannot let him be falling to sleep."

"I'll take your word for it," I said.

Marvin stopped hacking and was now dozing. Yuri clapped loudly to rouse him. "Do not fall to sleep, Marvin. You have to stay awake."

Outside, the wind was blowing so hard that it made the back doors tremble. Marvin mumbled something, then nodded off again. Ben was wringing his hands. "Oh God, man. This is bad," he whined. "This is really bad."

Yuri crouched down beside Marvin. "Sundance," he said, his accent dulling the word. "It is me. It is Butch."

Marvin opened his eyes. "Butch?" he whispered. "Butch, where are we?"

"Sundance, you have to be staying awake. We are making last stand."

"Okay, Butch," Marvin said with effort. "I won't fall asleep on you. I'll be right here at your side."

Ben's face brightened. Yuri gestured for him to get out the bottle of Coke for Marvin, then Yuri started rummaging through his suitcase.

"Good thinking," I said. Yuri shrugged. He was as surprised by what he'd said as I was.

"I have seen this movie *Butch Cassidy and the Sundance Kid*. It is good movie," Yuri said, handing me all of his clean socks and shirts. "I wanted to be cowboy when I was young. Did you want to be cowboy, James?"

"Sure," I said, and I suddenly remembered that, growing up, I'd had these recurring dreams in which I was a different cowboy every night: Billy the Kid, Roy Rogers, Jesse James. They were the most vivid dreams I'd ever had, Technicolor visions of yellow prairies, blue skies, galloping horses and fearsome shoot-outs. Each morning I woke up a hero. I hadn't thought of those dreams in years.

"Sometimes, when I was child," Yuri said, "I was taking rope and making . . . how do you call it?"

Ben glanced up from tending Marvin. "A lasso?"

"Yes, a lasso. And I would say, *Yee-ha*, like I was American cowboy."

"Yeah, I used to do that too," Ben chimed in. "But I could never get the lasso to work."

"Oh, it is simple," Yuri claimed proudly, closing his suit-case. "I could show you sometime. No problem."

"Really?" A grin spread across Ben's face.

Yuri took a shirt from my hand and began ripping it into strips.

"What are you doing?" I asked.

"Socks to clean blood. Shirts for his leg."

"I can make it, Butch." Marvin made an attempt to sit up, but fell back in pain and closed his eyes.

"Stay awake, Sundance," Yuri ordered, snapping his fingers. He tossed me one of his shirts, indicating for me to do as he was. "Quickly, James," he said softly, "We have not much time."

I began tearing up Yuri's shirt without even considering that, most likely, it was one of the only ones he owned.

"As a boy, my father gave me book on cowboys," Yuri said, gingerly threading the strips of cloth underneath Marvin's leg. "He bought it on black market for my birthday. I cannot guess how much it cost." Yuri laid a folded sweater on each side of Marvin's leg to brace it, then carefully tied the strips to immo-bilize the leg. Marvin was holding his breath to bare the pain. Yuri kept talking to distract him. "The book was having pictures of cowboys on horses and cowboys with guns, every kind of cowboy. It also tells how to make lasso. That is where I learned."

The memory of the book made Yuri smile. Then his smile dimmed.

"But one day, a boy from my village, Vassily Petrovich–his name I still remember–this boy stole my book. When I go to get it back, he says to me, 'If I cannot have it, you cannot.' Then he throws my book in fire."

We all held a sad silence until Ben protested, "That's not right, man. That was your book, man." He began pacing the hallway, lip quivering. "That was your book."

After a moment, Marvin said, "I'm real sorry about your book, Butch." They were the most sincere words I'd ever heard.

Yuri quietly finished binding Marvin's leg and began picking up the leftover scraps of cloth. I knelt to help him. "Thank you, James," he said, taking what remained of his shirt.

It seemed to me that I had never been less worthy of thanks in all my life. I had dragged Yuri into this situation and now he was bailing me out, a man whose last name I had never asked. At that moment, I was glad he didn't really know me, didn't even really know the language. Because if he had, he might have truly perceived how low I had let myself go. A raw draft was shuddering through the seams of the back doors and raising chills on my skin. I deserved to be cold, I thought, a lot colder than I was. It would have served me right for the way I had been acting. I owed Yuri, and I needed to pay him back.

"Oh no," Ben murmured.

A set of headlights swung across the dark, snowy street outside the rear entrance. Ben rushed over and pressed his face to the glass. He motioned me over. "That's them, Derek and his stupid sidekick. That's who did this to Marvin. I can tell by the car."

"They have nothing better to do than drive around in a snowstorm?" I asked.

"No," Ben replied.

A battered old Lincoln Continental was cruising up the street. Whoever was driving must have seen us because the car slowed down, then pulled over in front of the entrance, just feet away. I hoped that the glass doors were locked, but there was no way to be sure unless I pushed one, and by then, the man behind the wheel was staring right at me. His head was shaved bald and he had a brutal face, the kind that made me want to look away, but at the same time told me not to let him out of my sight.

Ben edged back from the doors, eyes frantic. Derek, the driver, cranked down his window.

"Long time no see, Benny boy," he shouted, loud enough to be heard through the doors. "How's that friend of yours?"

Ben's mouth fell open, but he was too afraid to answer.

"He's fine," I said. "Thanks for asking."

Derek raised a doubtful brow. "Oh yeah?"

"Sure. He's out roping some doggies right now."

I heard Yuri say my name, cautioning me, but I waved him off.

"Who are you, asshole?" Derek demanded. He sounded drunk.

"The name's James. Jesse James. Ever heard of me? I'm one of the toughest outlaws who ever lived. So I'd watch my step if I were you, kemosabe."

"This kid's mental," Derek said, elbowing the man in the passenger seat who I couldn't make out. "Did you see what I did to that old dude?" he asked me.

"Yup."

"And?" he sneered.

Yuri was patting Marvin's cheeks to keep him awake. He was fading fast. "James," Yuri urged, "I do not think . . ."

"Well, now that we've met," I said, hooking my thumbs into my belt loops, "I just want to know one thing."

"Oh, yeah?" Derek said. "What's that?"

"Do you wax that head of yours or pull the hairs out one by one?"

Derek's eyes narrowed. There was less than three feet of

sidewalk between us, and he appeared to be gauging how long it would take for him to get to me.

I crossed my arms, cocky, cavalier, egging him on. The adrenaline racing through me made my bones feel like wire. The hum of the fluorescent lights was as loud as an alarm. I lodged myself squarely in Derek's glare and said, "You ought to get a hat, *partner*. How can you even see yourself in a mirror with that high-beam shine?"

"James," Yuri repeated, his voice now brittle with tension.

I couldn't make up for what had happened to Marvin, for the beating he had braved, or for what had happened to Yuri, for the burning of his beloved book. The bad guys had not lost and the good guys hadn't won. The world was not right, it was not fair, and it was not clear. But I believed, for an instant, that I could make it so.

Derek said something to the passenger, then opened the car door slowly, letting it rock on its hinges. He was wearing heavy boots, and his leather jacket had been worn gray in places, as if by his muscles from the inside out. Snow was whipping through the air, pelting him, but he didn't seem to notice. It took two steps before we were toe to toe with only the door between us. Derek stood close enough to fog the glass with his breath.

"You think you're funny, kid?"

"No, I think you are. A big guy who beats up old men, that's as yellow as they come."

Derek motioned for his buddy to get out of the car. A barrel-chested man clad all in black, who was equally as big and doubly as frightening as Derek, joined him at the door. His silent, hulking presence personified every shadowy menace I had ever dreamed of or thought I could dream up. And now I was face to face with him.

It was a showdown, and I was outnumbered and outsized. My heart was stomping in my chest, my pulse thundering in my ears. I felt better than I had in weeks. But then the fear really kicked in, meaningful, comprehensible. I realized what I had gotten myself into, and my knees literally shook.

"You were saying, *partner?*" Derek snarled.

Then, in the reflection on the glass, I saw Yuri step up to my right side. Ben appeared on the left, forming a wall. We were smaller, skinnier, and far less intimidating, but there were three of us and two of them. Derek gave us the once-over and snickered, unimpressed.

I put my hands out by my hips as though ready to draw two imaginary guns and said, "What I was going to say was that you shouldn't polish that head of yours, partner. Because I've got to tell you, the glare is blinding me."

The force with which Derek hit the door was enough to send the three of us back a couple of steps, but the door didn't budge. It was locked. Derek shook it and kicked it and finally pounded the pane with his fist. There wasn't even a crack. The other man remained still, ready to back Derek up; he was unnervingly calm, with lifeless, unreadable eyes, and even with the door locked, that terrified me.

"Look!" Ben said. At the far end of the street a police car was rounding the corner. It was heading toward the bus station. "It's the cavalry!"

Derek backed off, cursing. "You're one lucky lunatic," he said, jabbing his finger at my face, then he bolted into his car. But the other man waited, staring me down. In his hollow eyes I saw my fate diverted, the punishment for all I had done avoided. And those eyes told me that I *had* been lucky, this time and so far, but that someday my luck might run out.

"Let's go. It's the cops," Derek commanded and the man returned to the car, then Derek peeled out, sending a flurry of snow from the car's roof into the air. The taillights made the snow glow red until the car was out of sight.

Yuri gave an audible sigh of relief, and Ben began whooping and cheering, "Chickens! Yellowbellys! Yee-ha!"

Yuri flagged down the police car. "They see us," he exclaimed. "They are coming."

"Butch?" Marvin whispered, his breath burbling. "Butch, did we win?"

"Yes, Sundance," Yuri said. "We won."

Once the emergency medics had wheeled Marvin out on a stretcher and the police had questioned us, somebody in the crowd of stranded passengers who had gathered around said that the next bus was pulling in and that we would be departing soon. The snowstorm was dying down. Yuri and I would make it to Baltimore by morning. He would get to see his family, and I would get to go home.

After that night, I never saw Yuri again, nor Marvin or Ben. I do not know what became of any of them, and for that, I am partly glad. Because in my mind I had created futures for them, whole lives, and they were doing well. Things had changed and gotten better. I never returned to Boston, not even to collect the things I had left. After Christmas, I did, however, send a package back there to Yuri, care of the school where we had met. In it were new shirts, some sweaters and socks, and a book about cowboys.

I am a professor now, teaching classes of my own in engineering, and spending most of my days on the kind of campus I'd ducked for so many years. At times, I catch myself studying my students while I lecture, noting whether they slouch or yawn and checking their eyes for any sign of that old sensation that had haunted me that winter. I do not think of that night in the bus station often, but occasionally the memory comes involuntarily, out of the blue, an unconscious reminder when I am losing faith in the world or myself. Then the thought returns as vivid as the cowboy dreams from my youth, and I feel honored to see the faces of those three men.

That night, after the crowd had cleared, Yuri and I were left to gather what was left of his things. I picked up his clothes and Yuri folded them as neatly as he could and repacked them. When I leaned over to get the last scrap of his clothing, something poked me in the back of the leg and I jumped, my nerves still keen and frazzled from all that had happened. But then I realized that it was only the lid of his suitcase, touching me in a place where I could finally feel it.

Acknowledgments

Grateful acknowledgment is made to the following publications in which some of the stories first appeared in slightly different form: *Retro Retro: A Modern Fiction Anthology*, published by Serpent's Tail ("Future Tense"); *Take Twenty: An Anthology of New Writing*, published by the Centre for the Creative and Performing Arts at UEA ("Unemployment"); *Red Cedar Review* ("Edith Drogan's Uncle Is Dead"); *Mid-American Review* ("Destination Known"); *Sonora Review* ("For Sale by Owner"). Acknowledgment is also made to the Hopwood and Haugh Prizes for Fiction presented by the University of Michigan.